SECRETS OF THE CANNABIS INDUSTRY

Chuck Allen Jr.

iUniverse LLC
Bloomington

SECRETS OF THE CANNABIS INDUSTRY

iUniverse books may be ordered through booksellers or by contacting:

iUniverse LLC
1663 Liberty Drive
Bloomington, IN 47403
www.iuniverse.com
1-800-Authors (1-800-288-4677)

ISBN: 978-1-4917-2748-5 (sc)
ISBN: 978-1-4917-2749-2 (hc)
ISBN: 978-1-4917-2747-8 (e)

Library of Congress Control Number: 2014904020

Printed in the United States of America.

iUniverse rev. date: 03/04/2014

Contents

Poems by Chuck Allen Jr.

For my wife Trish whose encouragement fanned a tiny spark. And a big thank you to our daughter Beverly for her computer skills and technical help.

PREFACE

I believe that in a free society people have the right to self-medicate; after all, that's why we have drugstores. Once a person becomes twenty-one years old, it's not the government's job to tell him what he can or cannot do with his body. It's also not the job of big businesses to regulate, behind closed doors, products that conflict or influence the profit margins of their stockholders. Companies that use lobbyists (lawyers) to influence politicians (lawmakers) to keep certain products from entering the free marketplace are participating in collusion at the highest level. They should be considered the worst kind of criminals, even worse than bank robbers or murderers, because they are stealing from the public coffers and killing businesses using false advertising and mass-media propaganda.

Lately it has been politically correct for the government to reverse its stance on marijuana laws. After seventy-five years of marijuana prohibition, the directors of the Off-Broadway show *The War on Drugs* now realize that the song-and-dance act has run its course, and the public isn't buying tickets anymore. But make no mistake about it, the government has no intentions of legalizing marijuana, because there's too much money to be made keeping it illegal. To me that's a good thing. Why would anyone in their right mind want the government to manage the cannabis industry? They can't balance the budget with the job they have! Besides, the cannabis industry is doing just fine without them. However, changing their stance on state and local laws is a giant step toward correcting some very bad decisions our politicians have been making for too many years. Making criminals out of normal taxpaying citizens, for possession of small amounts of marijuana, is not good for a free society. It disrupts the lives of families, neighborhoods, and businesses on almost every level.

Regardless of the decisions that our leaders are making with respect to the cannabis industry, there will always remain the opportunity for entrepreneurs to stand on their own two feet and keep the American dream alive. People who grow marijuana are the last pioneers in America. They are taking part in the last great adventure. They are the last proof that free people can stand on their own without relying on the government for support. But they must be careful, because our government doesn't want them to live without *their* control.

INTRODUCTION

This book is about the cannabis industry and the men and women who risked their family, friends, and freedom for their pursuit of happiness. Each chapter is a true story told to me by people whom I call pioneers in a subculture of entrepreneurs. Their courage and determination resulted in them becoming independent and financially successful in the cannabis industry. Names and locations have been changed to protect individual freedoms. My participation in these stories of adventure and intrigue was brief and financially disappointing, yet my willingness to be a part of the mystique of the cannabis industry encouraged me to write this book. Because of the collusion between politics and big business and the corruption in the leadership that followed the "war on drugs," I became infatuated with seeing to what lengths pundits and academia went in their support and willing participation in the mass-media propaganda schemes that still storm through America's homeland. There will be some pages where I may editorialize about why the cannabis prohibition has caused such a shameful mess in the kitchen of public opinions. But, I assure you, my words reflect the honest disgust and frustration caused by the people who are supposed to be truthful and honest in their dealings with the citizens who voted them into office in the first place.

You'll meet Professor Muzzo, who unknowingly helped one of his students achieve financial success by selling a popular fast-food item spiced with a secret ingredient. You'll learn about a postal employee with a secret garden in his basement. You'll find out about a Mexican connection from a bartender from Marin County, California. You'll read about my first and only outdoors marijuana grow that ended in total disappointment for me and financial success for my partner. You'll find out how one entrepreneur made a fortune selling franchises for indoor-growing opportunities. You'll discover how a Native American turned one of the most inhospitable desert regions in the world into a garden of cannabis delight. You'll meet the fireman's wife who owned a video store with extra-special movie-rental benefits. You'll meet the owners of a hemp store who were arrested for selling cannabis seeds. And you'll learn how a rock star and his friends successfully harvested the largest marijuana grow in US history.

My father was an officer in the military, and I grew up in a very traditional and conservative family where drugs were never mentioned, aside from alcohol or aspirin. When I graduated from high school in 1965, the cannabis industry was a concept whose time hadn't come yet. At least the general public wasn't aware of it on a massive scale. There were no drug-awareness programs, no buds being sold in the school parking lot, and no pot being smoked in the bathrooms. Marijuana wasn't a topic of conversation, because none of us knew what it was. We knew about other countries selling hemp for industrial profit, but we never made the connection that it was the distant cousin of the marijuana plant. It wasn't until years after high school that I smoked marijuana for the first time, and quite frankly, I wasn't that impressed with it. But my opinion changed when I moved to the west coast and started to party with the liberal sons and daughters of the very rich businessmen and politicians living in Marin County, California. They had the wealth and influence to buy the finest pot money could buy, and I learned quickly what it took to become a bud connoisseur in the free marketplace.

For over 160 years, the cannabis plant was a valued and trusted friend of the American people. Thirty-one consecutive presidents, including George Washington and Abraham Lincoln, didn't have a problem with the cannabis plant. It was the most valued commodity trading on the free market at that time. Then, in 1937, a group of wealthy politicians and businessmen went behind closed doors and conspired to destroy the hemp industry, in an effort to keep hemp products from competing with new synthetic products being introduced to the marketplace by their friends and colleagues. In the process of demonizing the hemp industry, they also took the opportunity to practice and establish new propaganda techniques on the American people. (In 1936 the IPA, or Institute for Propaganda Analysis, was established, and for the first time politicians and businessmen learned the value of seven propaganda methods that are still being used on unsuspecting citizens today.) The original group of conspirators are not alive anymore, but the propaganda system is still being used. Today's methods are more destructive because of the advancement of new mass-media technology, such as TVs, computers, cell phones, etc. They use a form of blatant or subliminal brainwashing that I call "social hypnotism," because they have managed to hypnotize a whole nation of people into doing whatever they want them to do, including: starting wars based on lies and false information, electing presidents with little or no experience in the business world, and declaring prohibition on the cannabis plant and then changing their minds when they discover new ways to tax it. The most dangerous thing about propaganda is that although some people can see reality, the majority of the population are taken in and see nothing of how they are being manipulated. Propaganda in the hands of politicians and big business could be a force for good, but in reality it's being used for satisfy greed and achieve control. They realize that it is an effective method of mass persuasion for them, but it's too bad for us, because it requires a rule of ethics that are being controlled by unethical people.

I wanted to write a book that shines the light on the positive things that the cannabis industry is doing in America today, including the cannabis-themed poems found at the end of each chapter. This book is also a great opportunity for you to hang out with people who have been around the block with the cannabis industry. Even if you feel you are the wisest person in the room, just try to listen to what this book is saying, because you just might learn something new different and exciting.

The cannabis industry is a complicated and compound subject that isn't easy to describe, but I feel it can be understood if the instruction stays within the boundaries of truth and honesty. This book just might smooth out some of the misinformation surrounding the subject and answer some of the questions that many people have acquired over the years. Consider it a romp down a hidden pathway, a peek behind closed doors, and a stroll through the secret gardens found only in the cannabis industry.

The truth about the cannabis industry has already been written by a man named Jack Herer in his book *The Emperor Wears No Clothes*. You can also find the truth on the Internet buried under a ton of misinformation and misunderstanding. There are millions of websites designed to inform you on historical facts and scientific evidence. There are congressional and Senate reports that have uncovered the truth about the cannabis plant, but they are stored in a warehouse unknown to you and me. There have been billions of wasted tax dollars spent on strongly held scientific opinions supported by even more costly research. I support you in your effort to find the truth about the cannabis industry, and I encourage you to read this book first, because it will help you sift through the fool's gold.

CHAPTER 1

Secrets of Why People Grow Cannabis

They are hardworking people with families to feed,
Who try to stay away from politics and greed.

I've had my finger on the pulse of the American consumer for over forty years. I've managed multimillion-dollar businesses, and as a licensed Realtor, I've helped hundreds of citizens achieve the American dream of property ownership. Part of my required education was to take state-run courses such as Real Estate Law, Financing, Appraisals, etc. One of the most important classes I took was a Real Estate Code of Ethics course designed to teach agents to be truthful in all aspects of the real-estate transaction. This brings me to the question, can man rule himself? When I started to fill out purchase and sale agreements and present them to other real-estate professionals, I began to realize that some of the biggest ethics violators in the business were themselves sitting on the board of ethics! It was easy for me to connect the dots between this one self-regulating organization and our own politicians who regulate themselves by removing term limits and giving themselves raises without demonstrating that they know how to balance the national budget. After ten years of dealing with self-centered, pompous, arrogant, dishonest, so-called professionals in real estate, I went back to managing restaurants, where dealing with customer complaints was at least somewhat honest.

Let's tell the truth with each other: there are no underground black-market marijuana growers lurking under a bridge somewhere conspiring to sell your children nightmares and monsters in the form of marijuana cigarettes. Those are progressive ideas and concepts sold to you through the mass-media propaganda machine to keep beneficial cannabis products off the free market. If you don't understand or believe what I just said, then you are part of the problem, not part of the solution. If you can't do the research and look up the historical facts on your own, then you're the kind of person who doesn't know how to rule himself, and you truly need to read this book. The cannabis industry is out in the open in full view of everyone who has a brain to think and eyes to see. One out of every six people you pass on the street supports the industry in one form or another. They either smoke pot or have smoked in the past. They either buy hemp products or know someone who has. I call this human behavior a subculture of independent thinkers who can rule themselves. It's a complex network of human beings who have created a viable industry based on courage, principles, and trust, producing a cannabis product that is manufactured in the privacy of their own homes or cultivated for their own use in the free marketplace. The buds from the marijuana plant are a $60 billion industry in the US—someone must like it. Over $30 billion of hemp products are consumed every year in the US. That's more than any other country in the world, but we can't manufacture it here—does that make sense? Why can't we reap the benefits for ourselves instead of giving the money to other countries? It feels as if we lost at the bargaining table somehow. Who is doing the negotiations on our behalf, some babbling idiot in Congress? Progressives know that if we were to find out that we can rule ourselves (become self-sufficient) there would be no need for one-world government, and they would lose their power over us. I know how that sounds, but it's as true as a turd in a punch bowl. That's why marijuana and hemp have been placed in the same wastebasket with UFOs and Bigfoot—to keep the power of information from getting into our minds. The cannabis industry can produce all the products we need to become self-sufficient. Don't take my word for it; do your own research if you truly want to make a difference. The reason our country is in bad shape is because we have let ourselves become too fat, too lazy, and too spoiled, and the progressives know this and have taken advantage of our good nature.

They don't want us to know that there is a group of free-thinking citizens making millions of dollars in the cannabis industry and contributing significantly to the global economy. What they want us to see instead is a neatly packaged propaganda video shown on the History Channel and designed to be sold to the public, so they can market their misinformation and make more money from the cannabis industry.

What they aren't saying is that those entrepreneurs who are making millions of dollars in the cannabis industry don't need the Supreme Court, the president, or the History Channel for permission to rule themselves. The truth has no agenda.

These stories I'm about to tell you are about real people, just like you and me, except that they have decided to change their lives for themselves and have stopped waiting for the government to do it for them. They are hardworking, God-fearing, taxpaying individuals who are standing on their own two feet and taking responsibility for their own actions, which brings us back to that age-old question, "Can man rule himself?" The answer is a resounding yes! It's being done every day, by millions of people with family and friends who haven't given up on their freedom and don't want their country to change into a socialistic or communistic system of government. Just a few more points, and we'll get to the idea of making a million dollars in the cannabis industry.

Today, 25 percent of our population is comfortable with big government or a benevolent dictator ruling their lives on every level. (There is no such thing as a benevolent dictator; that's progressive code talk for socialism.) Anyway, they want the government to provide them with food, shelter, clothing, and a job, if they have to work. They want the government to tell them when to get up and when to go to sleep, just like in the military. Life is much more comfortable and predictable for them and their family if someone else thinks for them. There are generations of our citizens who can't think for themselves anymore, and they will riot in the streets to protect their imagined guaranteed entitlements. Step by step, nudge by nudge, big government is grooming those citizens toward a one-world order, which is what the progressives like to call social democracy, but that's just code for communism. If you fall into this group, then growing cannabis to make a million dollars isn't something you would be doing, because you wouldn't be able to recognize the freedom of choice it takes to become an entrepreneur.

Before we get into the finer points of making money from growing marijuana, it's important to understand the necessity of thinking outside the box. It's a learned skill that requires the critical thinking that the government is trying to take out of the schools. The skill of "prejudging" problems or situations is absolutely critical in order to solve problems before they happen and has nothing to do with civil rights or the color of someone's skin. Entrepreneurs in the cannabis industry are developing the strong interpersonal skills that allow them to prejudge what big government and the "progressive" movement are trying to do with the American way of life.

When I was managing a produce department in a supermarket in northern California, I was amazed at the number of people who thought they knew more about tomatoes than everyone else. Because they had grown tomatoes in their backyard or on their patio, or because they had read a book or watched a video on the subject, they were experts capable of explaining how more much important their opinions were about tomatoes than were the manager's. Their enthusiasm only confirmed their lack of knowledge. But they still had the audacity to walk into a supermarket and insult the produce manager with their ignorance. They had never actually worked in a market before, but they still felt privileged enough to tell someone else how to run a business. They had never ordered from the supplier enough tomatoes to feed a village, a town, or a city with a population of tens of thousands of people. They didn't know about inventory price sheets, price markups, food cost, labor cost, storage procedures, rotating stock, refrigeration temperatures, display advertising, or dealing with the public. That's not to mention the years of on-the-job experience necessary to pass the state comprehensive exam to become a certified produce manager. Just as in the cannabis industry, there's more to it than just tomatoes. This is just another example of how you need to think outside the box if you intend to make a million growing pot. If you don't learn humility, your future in the cannabis industry will end tragically.

Have you ever wondered why there are so many cooking shows on TV with chefs being elevated to rock-star status? It's not because of their popularity; it's because the restaurant industry has the number-one failure rate of any business in America. People are made to believe that being a better cook will make the restaurant seem more successful. Actually, the TV shows are just another Madison Avenue scheme to sell more merchandise and more advertising. Being a certified chef will not make a restaurant more successful any more than hiring a professional dishwasher will attract more customers to the table. It's true that a good cook is the heartbeat of any restaurant, but it's equally true that not all chefs can cook. That's why most successful restaurant owners will hire an experienced manager who knows how to cook the menu, in case the cook gets sick or the manager has to fire him or her for some reason. It takes more than knowing how to cook to run a successful restaurant. What you see on TV is a performance, with cameras, scripts, directors, and an audience. It's a make-believe world that is rehearsed behind the scene for your enjoyment.

I once knew a chef who managed the kitchen at a very famous restaurant in downtown San Francisco. He had hundreds of loyal customers, and after twenty years of service he decided that he had had enough of working for someone else, so he took his life savings and opened his own business a few blocks away. Two years later, his restaurant went bust and left him flat broke, forcing him to return to the restaurant where he had started. The tough life lesson he had to learn was that knowing how to cook world-class food wasn't enough to ensure success. The same is true about the cannabis industry. If you want to make a million dollars growing pot, you'd better learn as much as you can about the marijuana business, because if you don't, the results could be devastating.

I suppose you're wondering what supermarkets and restaurants have in common with growing pot. The connection is very simple, yet complicated. It's called farming. You'd better know how to get your produce from the field to the table, because there's more to it than growing a few plants. It's just like any other agricultural product; you need to learn all the aspects of the business, including supply and demand and the code of ethics. If you don't, people in the business will not deal with you, and your million-dollar dream will be short-lived. I mean that with the greatest sense of urgency! Find yourself a mentor (which is not easy to do), find someone you can trust (which is not easy to do), and learn firsthand by doing a grow yourself (which is not easy to do). There are hundreds of self-help books, videos, and magazines out there to help you get started with seeds, equipment, and instructions. But that's not what this book is about. Just as in the restaurant and supermarket industries, there are formulas for success, and those people who find out what those formulas are will have a better chance of succeeding than those who don't. Those formulas are what this book is about, so pay attention while you're reading, because the secrets to your success are hidden in the pages of this book.

When you decide that growing marijuana is something that you want to do, I advise that you start small and that you keep it confidential. Growing outside when you live within city limits is not a great idea, even if you grow only one plant. There are so many variables for getting caught that it's beyond listing. I suggest that you start indoors with a closet grow, or maybe in a corner of the basement or garage. Learn how to deal with anxiety and paranoia and the telltale aroma of mature buds calling out to your neighbors when you open the front door. After a few small grows, you'll began to understand how many plants it will take to grow one pound, two pounds, etc. You will also realize along the way how much moisture is lost in the drying process.

On your quest for growing a million dollars' worth of buds, you'll have to make a crossroads decision: do you make money in small increments or grow big in a short time? You can only grow so many pounds in your basement without alerting your neighbors or the electric company (not to mention the police, with their new heat-detecting devices). There are hundreds of thousands (maybe millions) of entrepreneurs making a comfortable living supplementing their income by growing two pounds every four months. That's a nice-size business that shouldn't attract attention; you would only be using four 1,000-watt lights and one fluorescent bulb. (Keep in mind that you would have to grow four pounds to get two pounds of dried buds.) The formula should look something like this. An average grow is 120 days, or three times a year. An average bulk rate price is $2,000 per pound.

2 lb. x 3 grows a year = 6 lb.
6 lb. x $2,000 per pound = $12,000 per year tax-free
$12,000 x 10 yrs. = $120,000 tax-free

If you decide to sell your pounds by the ounce, your profit will increase, but your number of deals will increase too, increasing your chances of getting caught. There are 16 ounces in a pound, so 96 ounces in 6 pounds. Average price for 1 ounce is $360.

$45 x 8 = $360 (Divide the ounce into eighths, at $45 each.)
$360 x 16 ounces = $5,760 per pound
$5760 x 6 lb. =$34,560 per year, tax-free
$34,560 x 10 yrs. = $345,600 tax-free
$34,560 x 20 yrs. = $691,200 tax-free
$34,560 x 30 yrs. = $1,036,800 tax-free. Million-dollar goal!

Not bad money for working part-time in the basement of your home! Your average postal worker makes $50,000 a year; that's $500,000 in ten years, and a cool million in twenty years. If I had to choose between the two jobs, I wouldn't be working for the government. But that's where your values and principles come into play, and every entrepreneur has to make that choice.

If you decide to grow outdoors, that's a different animal altogether. Growing just a few plants on your deck, on your patio, in your flowerbed, or with your backyard vegetable garden will get you busted just the same as an indoor closet grow will—probably faster. There are obvious problems that require different rules. The number-one rule when growing *anywhere* is that you must have privacy or create a sense of privacy, also known as seclusion, isolation, solitude, and/or remoteness. If you choose to grow inside the city limits, you have already broken the first rule, because you aren't living in a remote location. If you're brave enough to think that no one can see over your fence, go for it. If you think none of your neighbors can see your back deck or patio, go for it. If you honestly believe that no one will smell your award-winning buds two blocks away, go for it. If your strongly held opinion tells you that the police would never enter your backyard without permission, then go for it. You deserve exactly what's going to happen to you. There's an old saying in Alabama: you have to be smarter than the cat—and damn few people are!

Some of the other problems you might encounter growing outdoors in the city limits are ants, beetles, grasshoppers, rabbits, skunks, deer, squirrels, and kids looking for lost Frisbees. Cats love pot plants. They think it's catnip, and dogs can dig up a plant faster than you can say *holy shit!* One thing I can say for sure: growing pot around the outside of your house will not produce a million bucks, only a million ways to get fucked.

Nevertheless, if you have courage, determination, and balls the size of Texas, growing a few plants for personal use in your veggie garden is a good way to start to understand what it takes to grow a little pot outdoors. (You might even make some extra money.)

There are entrepreneurs who are making big bucks inside the city limits using warehouses and commercial buildings, but they are the exception, not the rule. Although I've never been involved with a grow on that level, I've known people who have. When I was selling real estate, I had clients who bragged about what certain buildings had been used for before they had come up for sale. Commercial businesses that deal with the manufacturing of heavy equipment—like steel beams, tractor trailers, ships, tugboats, trucks, farm equipment, etc., etc.—almost always require a special permit to use large quantities of electricity to operate their welders and heavy machinery.

The reason why these big-time growers are so successful is easy to explain but hard to do. Once again, isolation and security are important, and most of the company employees will not be aware of any secret garden on the property. The growers first pick a grow site, usually in the basement or on the top floor, but sometimes in a restricted or hazardous area somewhere on the property. These gardens are almost always maintained by family members or close family friends who dress and look like any other employee. Power is diverted to the grow site, and the air-conditioning system is designed to circulate the smell of the buds in with the exhaust fumes from the heavy equipment being used on the regular job site. These big-time growers are very successful and have made millions of tax-free dollars, but not without big-time risks. (You may call them criminals, but I call the entrepreneurs.) Almost always when these secret gardens are busted, it's because of informants (disgruntled ex-wives, ex-husbands, ex-lovers, etc.) and very rarely from undercover police officers as you see on TV. The power companies aren't concerned about how much energy is being used, because that's why they are in the business, to sell electricity. As long as a business has the necessary permits, there's no reason for the power company to be suspicious, unless they are contacted by the authorities who themselves have been contacted by an informant. There are occasions when building inspectors and health inspectors pose a risk to the secret business, but those inspections are almost always known well in advance, giving the owners enough time to clear the grow site. The most difficult problems that the entrepreneurs will face is something I call the X factor: incidents that occur out of the blue, like fire alarms going off accidentally, 911 calls, broken water lines, electrical fires—anything that would unexpectedly bring in the police, fire marshal, or building inspector.

Let's look at a formula that might apply to one of these big time commercial growers, based on the use of one hundred 1,000-watt lights, one hundred 600-watt lights, and 50 fluorescent lights. The grower could expect fifty pounds of dried buds three times a year at a bulk price at $2,000 a pound.

50 x 3 = 150 pounds per year
150 x $2,000 = $300,000 per year
$300,000 x 5 yrs. = $1.5 million tax-free

This formula could easily be doubled, and probably has been with the addition of a second room or building. Making a million dollars growing indoors in the cannabis industry can be done, has been done, and will continue to be done, as long as there are people who are willing to rule themselves.

Let's change directions for a while and talk about the American farmer and his agricultural business. Do you honestly believe that farmers aren't growing marijuana in between the corn rows—especially in states where there are no surveillance planes and helicopters searching for the evil herb? Now, I'm not saying *every* farmer is doing it, but what I am saying is that there are some farmers who are supplementing their income and making a healthy living by doing it. There are more than a few who are actually getting rich, and most Americans aren't even thinking about it. They can use barns and outbuildings to grow indoors, and they have generators to supply their own power. Some farms are completely off the grid and prefer it that way. Their only concern would be an occasional agricultural inspector or a lost hunter who wanders into a secret garden hidden in the middle of a one-thousand-acre corn field.

It really doesn't matter whether you choose to grow indoors or outside; there are basically twelve considerations in getting started:

1. Seclusion and security (no talking and no showing)
2. Light source (natural or artificial)
3. Water source (with fluoride or without)
4. Seeds (cheap or expensive)
5. Soil and nutrients (artificial fertilizers or organic)
6. Correct temperature (indoors or outside)
7. Growing vegetation (solid soil or liquid)
8. Flowers and blooms (with or without seeds)
9. Harvesting (drying and manicuring)
10. Transportation (moving buds from one place to another)
11. Production (weighing and packaging)
12. Sales (bulk or street)

It's also important to understand what to do with your cash once you actually get it in your hands. The IRS has long arms and sticky fingers, so don't make any deposits larger than $10,000, and don't keep a safe-deposit box.

When I was in college, I had an appointment with the dean of the Behavioral Science Department at San Francisco State. When I arrived at his office he was still at lunch, and I read a sign on his door that said, "There are three kinds of lies in the world: little white lies that don't hurt anyone, big black lies that hurt everyone, and then there are statistics." When I was finally seated in front of his desk, I asked him about the sign on his door. He explained that little white lies are like the Easter Bunny and Santa Claus: they really don't hurt anybody; big black lies are like infidelity and gossip that hurt everyone; and statistics are the worst lies of all, because they are being created by law firms (lobbyists) to reflect and camouflage the special interest being sold to the voting public. The dean used voter pamphlets as an example. Pundits go to law firms to create voter-information sheets, and the lawyers create the explanations for what the voter is voting for. Oftentimes the explanation is designed to make the voter think they are voting *yes* on a particular measure when, because of the wording, they are actually voting *no*, which is the complete opposite of their beliefs. I've often experienced this myself while reading a question in the voting booth: "What in the hell does this question mean?"

The point of this story is that we don't know who to trust anymore. Doctors are dealers for the pharmaceutical companies, lawyers are bought and sold to the highest bidder, politicians are in the pockets of the special interest groups, and the government is in bed with big business. The Democrats don't trust the Republicans and the Republicans don't trust the Democrats. And the independents don't trust a two-party system. We can't trust the media to report the news accurately and fairly, because they're too busy telling a story that reflects the view point of the CEO or the owner of the station.

If our leaders can destroy the most beneficial plant in the world, what else are they destroying? Could it be the republic, the Constitution, academia, the economy, health care, Social Security, our religion, and the principles and values that built this great nation? If you don't know or understand that cannabis is the most beneficial plant on the face of the earth, then you need to find out for yourself and learn something new in your life. Don't take my word for it. Do your own research, and stop depending on the news to tell you the truth, because television is part of the problem, not the solution. Academia has failed to take the microphone and set the record straight because tenure has given them the right to be idiots and traitors. That's why I have so much admiration and respect for the cannabis industry—because they are a subculture of individuals fighting for their freedom, and they aren't afraid to stand up on their own two feet and rule themselves

The New Entrepreneurs

By Chuck Allen Jr.

In a few short weeks it will be harvest time;
Most of the growers have a lot on the line.
They are hardworking people with families to feed,
Who try to stay away from politics and greed.

They are skilled in the arts of growing outdoor,
But they enjoy hydroponics a little bit more.
In a few short days, the buds will be cured,
And a year's worth of income hopefully secured.

In a few short seasons, a free man can stand
On his own two feet and live off the land;
That's the dirty little secret they don't want you to know;
The cannabis industry will continue to grow.

CHAPTER 2

Secrets of the Tiburon Shuffle

The girls would be rocking with no shoes on their feet;
The guys would be toking in the middle of the street.

Back in the '60s and '70s, when I was a wild young man, I smoked enough pot to sink the *Titanic* several times. Unlike most critics of the weed, I remember those days with crystal clarity. Most of the pot coming into our town was coming from Mexico; we called it Mexican brown or commercial shit. It was okay pot, but we had to smoke a lot of it just to get sleepy. We mostly smoked it because it was cheap, but it was also better than nothing. Every once in a while, some Yucatan Gold or Panama Red would surprise the local tokers with a sample of what pot was supposed to taste like, and it was during those times that we had to move fast if we wanted to score something special.

I was at a volleyball game at the Tiburon Cove Park when I smoked my first puff of Skunk Bud. It was handed to me by a friend of mine who is now a lawyer putting people behind bars for doing the same things we were doing back then. Anyway, this fresh new pot was better than anything I had ever smoked before, and fortunately for all of us tokers, it was grown in the Emerald Triangle of northern California. Even today the seeds from those plants are producing some of the most sought-after buds in the world. It wasn't until that moment, at that park, that I realized what smoking marijuana was truly all about. People who know marijuana will understand; people who don't know will never understand, and that will always be the difference in trying to understand cannabis. Those self-proclaimed experts in their white lab coats, subjecting monkeys to a hundred marijuana cigarettes a day just to prove that marijuana will make a monkey sick, are nothing but babbling idiots who don't know their ass from a hole in the ground. The only truth they ever discovered was the paycheck given to them by the taxpayers—who in return received nothing but misinformation and fairy tales.

When I was in my early twenties, I found myself living in Tiburon, California, which today is one of the richest communities in America. It's located west of the Golden Gate Bridge, in Marin County, which is also one of the richest counties in the United States. But back in the early '70s, Tiburon was a sleepy bedroom town where cows still grazed in the hills and the rich acted as if they weren't. For twelve years I lived downtown in a one-bedroom apartment above a pizza parlor on Main Street. I was what some residents considered the local hippie; others referred to me as "that colorful character with the long hair and beard." I worked at a variety of jobs during this time, just for the privilege of living in such a beautiful and romantic place.

I worked primarily for two rich and powerful families. One owned a paint contracting company, and the other owned most of downtown Tiburon. Can you conceptualize what it's like to work for a family that owns the town where you live—supermarkets, banks, gas stations? It was like dancing on the edge of greatness but being a very poor dancer. It was like screwing the homely daughter and knowing in your heart that you would never marry her. Being around all that wealth made me realize I was never going to inherit a fortune or hit the lottery and if I was going to be rich, I would have to do it on my own, with my own courage and determination.

Tiburon is an old railroad town that was transformed with gift shops and mansions and then presented to the world like pearls on the neck of a beautiful woman. During the week she offered comfort and grace, but on the weekend you could glimpse her undressed, blowing in the wind. And sometimes, if you were lucky, you would see nothing at all.

When I wasn't working construction or painting houses for one family, I was working in a restaurant or supermarket for the other family. There were times in between those jobs that I went out on my own and did something different for myself, like working as the harbormaster for the second-oldest yacht club on the west coast, or starting my own business called Chuck-a-Truck Moving and Hauling.

During this process of working for wealthy people in a wealthy community, I made friends with a lot of folks who liked pot and didn't mind spending money to have their smoke. By osmosis, I kinda, sorta invented something I called the Tiburon shuffle, where I would shuffle over to one friend's house and pick up some money, then shuffle over to another friend's house and buy a pound of pot, then shuffle back to my house to make sure the weight was accurate, and then shuffle back to the first friend's house to deliver the pound of buds. I know this is hard to believe, but in the beginning I wasn't paid to do the Tiburon shuffle, because back in those days (the early '70s), the pounds of marijuana that came across the border from Mexico arrived here in kilos (2.2 lb.), and dealers would basically split the kilo in half with their hands, because scales were expensive and people were going to jail just for having a set in their houses.

Anyway, when I got the pound back to my place, it would always be two or three ounces over, and I never had to spend money to buy my own pot—*plus*, at parties I was the person who had something to smoke when everyone else was out, making me a very popular guy in town.

Back in those days, pounds cost between $400 and $600, and eventually I started to add an additional $100 because of the chance I was taking shuffling from one place to the next. I never sold anything less than a pound, and I always had extra money in my wallet.

The really good pot that was coming in from Hawaii, Jamaica, Thailand, and Mendocino was almost always broken down into ounces and eighths. Ounces were hard to find, but not impossible, because people with money didn't care about the price of an ounce. They weren't looking to resell; they were looking to party.

Thanks to the war on drugs, today the cost of a pound has increased tenfold. A pound of Skunk Bud back in 1975 cost $800. Today, the same buds will cost $8,000 when broken down into ounces and eighths. Brokers who are buying entire crops at the end of a harvest are generally paying $2,000 to $2,500 a pound and then selling to a dealer for $3,500. The dealer then breaks the pound into ounces and makes $8,000 a pound selling ounces for $500 each. ($500 x 16 ounces = $8,000 − $3,500 = $4,500 profit.) As you can calculate for yourself, there's plenty of money to go around for everybody. That's why the California marijuana initiative in 2010 failed, because the people of the state understood that when the government got involved in regulating and taxing public businesses they always screwed it up. Just look at the post office, health care, and Social Security if you need examples. Contrary to what you may have heard on the news, it had nothing to do with the people rejecting marijuana and everything to do with them rejecting the government. The cannabis industry is an $60 billion-dollar-a year industry that's working just fine without the government's sticky fingers trying to take money that doesn't belong to them. In fact, they have done everything in their power to keep the industry suppressed, and now they want to get in on the profits, and the people have said *no!* It goes back to the founding fathers, the Constitution, and the great experiment, "Can Man Rule Himself?" And the people of California proved that they can.

Have you ever asked yourself: Why is the government so desperately fighting a drug war that they have no hope of winning? It's because they would have to admit to three things: that they are fools, that they made a mistake, and that they can't control every aspect of a person's life in a free society. People are beginning to wake up and realize that if the government gets too big it will turn on them and take control of every part of their lives, just as in a communist country. I wish and pray that it's not too late. As long as the cannabis industry is strong and healthy, it should give every American a hopeful sign that the individual can still stand on his own and rule himself. If you think I'm crazy, then you're part of the problem and seriously need to educate yourself on the difference between propaganda and public relations. If, by some miracle, you discover that they are both one and the same, then you might be on the right path to understanding. This pot business is a lot more complicated than you thought, isn't it?

For more than twelve years I did the Tiburon shuffle, and I think the story is important. If you're thinking about making a million dollars in the cannabis industry, you need to know every aspect of the business, from start to finish. If you don't, your heart and soul will not be in it, and somewhere along the line your integrity will come into question, and someone will get hurt—probably you or someone you love.

There are hundreds, perhaps thousands, of books, magazines, and videos you can buy to help you get started. In some states there are college classes you can take that will teach you the fundamentals, but eventually you'll have to grow some balls and go out there and do it yourself.

Let's fast-forward 120 days to a time when you have a pound of freshly dried buds. How are you going to sell it? What are going to do with the money? At the one-pound level, you'll probable smoke some of it, sell some of it to your friends, and use the money to buy a TV or some new clothes. But this book isn't about how to grow a pound of pot; it's about getting to a place that will change your life forever and take you to a different level of understanding. The ball game changes from the little league to the pros, where people try to throw you in prison for long periods of time, and other people will try to rip you off or perhaps kill you for what you have or know. Trust is something you earn with truthful behavior, not good intentions. The prisons and cemeteries are full of people with good intentions. No one does it on his or her own, so find someone you can trust and form a bond of courage and determination. Then take responsibility for your actions.

Back in the late '60s and most of the '70s, I wore my hair long and kept a neatly trimmed beard. I wore bellbottom jeans with brown dress boots. Vary rarely would you see me wearing a T-shirt; I preferred solid-color long-sleeve cotton shirts. As I said before, I drank beer, smoked my share of the magical herb, went to rock concerts, and said the occasional "cool, man" or "far out." Once I took a girlfriend to see a blues festival at the UC Berkeley campus, and after the show, before the crowd left, some leftist speakers took over the podium and started shouting radical words about freeing the Chicago Seven prisoners being held someplace. Before we knew it, there was a full-blown riot going on, with police dogs, horses, and teargas explosions in the streets. Hundreds of uniformed police officers came marching toward us, shoulder to shoulder, with shields and batons at the ready. People were throwing rocks and bricks through storefront windows, but to this day I couldn't tell you what a pawnshop owner had to do with the Chicago Seven.

But even having done all that wild and crazy stuff, not once did I ever consider myself a hippie. And I'll tell you something else: there was a popular song by Steppenwolf back in those days, called "The Pusher" and some of the words were, "God damn the pusher man," but I have to be honest and tell you that not once did I ever think that doing the Tiburon shuffle had anything to do with being a pusher man. I always thought the song was about pharmaceuticals. Anyway, I suppose you're wondering what hippies and riots have to do with the cannabis industry. Well, in a way, everything.

Those people who had the courage and determination to take their grievances to the streets in demonstrations were the same ones who put a stop to the war in Vietnam. They were the ones who discovered that change comes from within and that they didn't need to depend on the government for permission to make a difference in their lives or the lives of their children. I know it sounds crazy, but you can't talk about a simple plant without talking about a simple-minded government. It wasn't just those hippies who were marching in the streets; it was their families, their friends, and their loved ones, who maybe didn't understand or agree with everything that they were doing. But somehow they knew in their hearts that something important was happening in our country, and that maybe, just maybe, our leaders didn't have our best interests in mind and could even be our enemy. Those are the people who started the cannabis industry, and those are the entrepreneurs who are once again saving this country from itself.

We weren't paying attention to what was going on in Vietnam. (It's still happening today in the Middle East.) Everyone thought that the military was running the show, but they weren't. It was our progressive politicians, who thought they knew more about winning a war than the generals did. So, instead of bombing bridges, warehouses, boat harbors, and manufacturing plants, they had the Air Force bombing the jungle, away from the cities and the training camps and the Viet Cong headquarters, so no one would get hurt.

After all, you can't have innocent men, women, and children getting killed in a war; someone's feelings might get hurt. The media wasn't paying attention either; they were too busy telling a good story. Academia wasn't paying attention; they were too busy trying to win the war on words. (That's still going on today.) The church wasn't paying attention because they were too busy supporting God's war. After all, we can't have the communists taking over the Christian world.

I think by now you should be starting to realize that the war on drugs isn't about the cannabis industry; it's about the government winning the psychological war of words, so *they* can control a nation's psyche, through propaganda and misinformation. If you think this is just some sort of wacko conspiracy theory, then you don't need to be trying to grow pot in the woods to make a million dollars; you need to keep doing what you're doing, so you can keep getting what you're getting. Entrepreneurs don't listen to people or governments who tell them, "No, you can't do that! You must think this way, not that way." It's best that you learn the truth now, before you go stumbling around in the woods looking for a million-dollar deposit for your bank account.

In the world of law enforcement, the cannabis industry is called the *black market*, and it's a place where underground activity goes undetected and uncontrolled by them, and they spend hundreds of billions of dollars of taxpayers' money to build their *own* black market, called the Drug Enforcement Administration, or DEA.

In the real world, the cannabis industry is called the marijuana industry, because most people consider hemp cannabis, and they don't smoke hemp. It's a twisted inside joke, because there is no hemp industry anymore, get it? Marijuana and hemp come from the same cannabis plant but with different seeds. It's like comparing the corn we eat at the dinner table to the corn we feed to cattle: same corn plant, different seeds, different results. Our illustrious leaders are in collusion with big business and the scientific community to keep the cannabis plant demonized in the minds of the American people. Don't take my word for it; look it up, do your own homework, educate yourself. But I strongly suggest that you not grow marijuana for a living unless you understand the difference.

When I was doing the Tiburon shuffle, I didn't ask or care about how my friends were getting the pounds that they were selling to me. To tell the truth, I really didn't want to know, because if something went wrong, I wouldn't have any information to give to the authorities. All I cared about was buying and delivering the product safely.

The first time one of my connections took me into his confidence and told me where he got his pounds, I was working for a very prestigious yacht club in the Bay Area. This man's father was one of the entrepreneurs who had started the industry that installed sound systems in elevators, supermarkets, malls, restaurants, and many other businesses across the country and around the world. When his father died, he inherited at fortune at the age of thirty-two and had more money than he knew what to do with. First he tried golf, then tennis, then drinking, then women, and after he had exhausted all those hobbies, he discovered sailing. He bought a beautiful new forty-two-foot ketch under the condition that the saleswoman would teach him how to sail. Long story short: after a few years of instruction, they got married and spent the rest of their life sailing the Caribbean. It was while they were in Jamaica that they discovered the beautiful island queen, marijuana. They brought a few pounds back to the States and started sharing the goodness with more and more friends, who encouraged them to go back to the islands and start their own import business. They built a hidden compartment in the galley of their boat and brought back 200 pounds (about the average weight of a grown man), making $400,000 each trip. (200 x $2,000 = $400,000.)

I had seen this man around the yacht club many times, and I knew he was a member of the board of directors. He enjoyed socializing with guests and visitors and often struck up conversations with me. One day, I was working on the dock in front of his boat, installing new Styrofoam logs under the planking, and he asked me if I would like a cold beer. He said that his wife was visiting friends for a few days and he wondered if I would like to go sailing after work. From that day on we became friends, and we often sat on the deck of his boat drinking beer and watching the skyline of the bay change colors. It wasn't too long before the topic of conversation came around to my favorite subject, marijuana, when he asked me if I partook of the magical herb. The grin on my face gave him my answer, and we shared a bowl of some of the best weed I had ever tasted. He said that his wife's parents had given them a home in Sausalito but they preferred to keep their boat at the yacht club because they loved the small town atmosphere better. Then he gave me a bag of buds and asked if I would keep an eye on their boat while they were away. Thus, our friendship went to a new level.

From time to time I would see him walking from the parking lot to the boat with a well-dressed man who looked like he could be a lawyer or CEO for some major corporation. When they returned to the car, the man would be carrying a canvas bag, which he would place in the trunk. Normally, people don't pay attention to that kind of activity, but I'd done the Tiburon shuffle too many times not to recognize the dance.

One stormy afternoon, I was checking berths and cleat lines for damage, and he asked me to come aboard his boat for a cup of hot coffee. I went down into the galley and took a seat next to the table. As we sat there drinking our coffee, he asked me if I had ever noticed him talking with a well-dressed man in the parking lot, and of course I said that I had. As it turned out, that man was his brother-in-law, and also the family lawyer who was taking care of some last-minute paperwork for the music company. The brother-in-law was being transferred to the East Coast and had paid a short visit to say goodbye.

While we were listening to the rain beat heavily on the galley roof and sipping the last of our coffee, my friend stood up and took the cushion off a teak bench that was built in to the wall next to the gas stove. He pressed down on one corner of the bottom plank, and the board popped up. Then he motioned for me to take a look inside the chest. What I saw was ten one-pound packages of dark-green buds, neatly stacked, five in a row. He said that he had been trying to talk to me about this for about a month but hadn't known how to start the conversation.

I couldn't believe my eyes! I had never seen so much pot in my life. It was something that the average human being didn't get to see in a lifetime; I still dream about those pounds every once in a while. He lowered the plank again and placed the cushion back on top of the bench. Then we both returned to the table and started grinning at each other in silence. He said, "I know this is an awkward moment, but I was wondering if you might know someone who wanted to buy a pound or two?" I enthusiastically said yes and told him that I would need some samples and a few days to collect the money. He said that he wanted me to be his partner in the Bay Area, because his brother-in-law had left him in a lurch, and he thought I was trustworthy and dependable. He would sell the pounds to me for $500 each, and I could keep whatever I made above that price. I was tap dancing in heaven. I sold everything he had in a week and made a few tax-free dollars.

I'm sure there are people still alive today who remember those buds that were brought to Marin County in the fall of 1975. Once or twice a year my partner sailed into the Bay Area and brought with him some of the best Jamaican buds ever sold on the West Coast. That business relationship we formed lasted for over five years, until I got married and moved out of the area. But that's a perfect example how trust and confidence is built in the cannabis industry; when people hear the hand of opportunity knocking on their door, they either recognize the secret knock or they don't.

For Those Who Would Dare

By Chuck Allen Jr.

I didn't call myself a hippie back in the seventies.
My hair was long and my jeans had holes in the knees;
I had a good job and I drove a blue truck.
Nobody could say I was down on my luck.

Friday-night parties with beer and some herb;
No one could say a discouraging word.
The girls would be rocking, with no shoes on their feet;
The guys would be toking in the middle of the street.

The cops would be looking and sniffing the air;
Driving home had to be handled with care.
But once we got home, and the front door was latched,
I went to my desk drawer and pulled out the stash.

I had a blue couch that would comfortably seat four;
The rest of my friends would take to the floor.
A singer with a guitar was making her point,
While I passed to my left a spicy new joint.

Those Friday-night parties that we had in Marin,
Back in the seventies when we were young again,
Are memories I treasure from those golden days,
Even if the faces are a brown-yellow haze.

But I do remember, from that fog of the past,
When the freedom of a country would always last,
And a general good feeling of smoking with care
Was acceptable behavior for those who would dare.

CHAPTER 3

Secrets of the Mexican Connection

Back in the '70s, it was understood,
We bought our pot wherever we could.

This is another story about confidence and trust in the cannabis industry. It happened when I was bartending for a popular restaurant in downtown Mill Valley. I was good friends with a waiter who worked in a different restaurant down the street. He was a Mexican citizen with a green card, and he liked it that way. He spoke beautiful English with a Mexican accent, and the tourists and locals always asked to be seated in his section so he could be their waiter. We both lived in the same apartment building and often played poker and went fishing together. He didn't smoke, drink, or chase women like I did, but he didn't seem to mind my crazy behavior. One day he told me that he was going on vacation for a week, and he asked me if I would like to meet his parents in Mexico. How could I say no? So a few days later, I and my girlfriend of the time booked a flight to Guadalajara, and within hours we were walking the streets of a small fishing village on the banks of Lake Chapala.

With the tips my friend was making at the restaurant, he had managed to build a beautiful ranch-style home for his parents in their hometown, complete with tropical gardens and peacocks. He had also bought his father a small cafe bar with two pool tables, so he would have some income. His family was much admired and very popular in the village.

Unfortunately for me, I came down with Montezuma's revenge and spent the first two days in Mexico standing in the shower spewing from both ends, but my girlfriend had a wonderful time being escorted around town by my good friend. On the third day of our visit I felt much better, and we took a short trip over to the coast and stayed overnight at a small tourist town called Manzanillo, which is located about sixty miles south of Puerto Vallarta. What a beautiful place this was, with its crescent-shaped beach and small fishing boats bringing fresh shrimp to sell to the people waiting on the beach. The large open market with its fresh fruits and vegetables was the heartbeat of the village activity.

As my girlfriend and I sat on the beach, enjoying the sun and surf, we noticed a black man riding a white horse up and down the shoreline, apparently looking for someone. There weren't more than twenty people on the beach, and it didn't take him long to ride over and stop in front of our blanket. He was tall, muscular, and very handsome. He wore a wide, friendly smile. He introduced himself by mentioning that he was friends with my friend from Mill Valley, and he invited us back to his house, which was only a short distance down the beach, for lunch. We spent a very pleasant afternoon listening to him play the guitar and sing songs in a wonderful operatic voice. He had been born in Oakland and raised in San Luis Obispo. He'd moved to Guadalajara five years ago, with a recording contract to sing American rock 'n' roll songs in Spanish. He toured with his band, doing concerts all over Mexico, and his songs were doing very well on the radio.

It was after a few beers and a couple of tokes from some local weed that I found out the real reason I had been invited to Mexico. Our new friend knew about my Tiburon shuffle and admired my ability to move quantities of product. Unknown to me, my waiter friend was engaged to the sister of one of his band members. The groom's father owned a farm back in the hills, not far from the coast, and had been growing marijuana for many years. They wanted to know if I would be interested in selling pounds in Marin County. I told him the Mexican brown shit was flooding the market, and prices weren't very good. He told *me* that he had bought $40,000 worth of Humboldt Skunk Bud seeds, and a fresh crop of new product would be ready to harvest in about thirty days. He assured me that the product would be brought across the border safely and delivered to the Bay Area with no complications. His explanation was that he had a friend in the construction business who had access to a sand and gravel pit not far from the border. The marijuana would be placed in the back of an empty dump truck, covered with a plastic tarp, and hidden under tons of sand or gravel. The inspection stations were so crowded with bumper-to-bumper traffic, and the truckers were never asked to pull over to dump their loads. It was too time consuming and labor intensive for them to even think about; besides, not all dump trucks were carrying marijuana. The complaints would be staggering. Once the trucks got across the border, they drove to another construction site, just north of Los Angeles, and the product was loaded into vans and driven to a farm in Petaluma, from there the buds were stored in a hidden compartment under bales of hay. All I had to do was drive to the farm, pick up some samples, and return with the money. The owner of the farm was another family member who would make sure that everything was cleared before I arrived.

Just a few more comments about transporting cannabis products—I don't care if it's across town or across country. When you're in the cannabis business, you'd better have your shit together. You may or may not realize this, but 80 percent of prison offenses are drug related, either for possession or for paraphernalia. People make stupid human mistakes that most likely could have been avoided. We've all gone out to dinner and had too many glasses of beer and then gotten in the car and driven home. We've all gone to a parties and had a few puffs and then realized that we were still ten miles away from home. Those are stupid human mistakes that are made by millions of people every day.

If you expect to make a million dollars in the cannabis trade, you'd better be smarter than the cat! When you're in a car, I don't care whether it's moving or not, you don't have marijuana on your person—not in a baggie, not a joint, not a pipe, not a roach, not a seed, not on your cloths, not in your hair, and not in your eyes—and nothing means *nothing* pot related. Don't think you can hide something in your underwear, in your socks, in your hat, in your cigarette pack, or inside your bra, because it's been tried and failed time and time again. If you've got a secret garden growing in your closet at home, you'd better not be stupid enough to think that hiding marijuana under the backseat of your car will keep you safe, because that's another stupid human mistake that could land you in prison for a long time. Police officers are well trained, and they have dogs that are well trained too.

If you think profiling is illegal, you deserve to go to jail. Police officers are trained to observe and report; what do you think the definition of the word *observe* is? It's code for "profiling"; they are looking for suspicious activity, or signs of illegal behavior. If a cop pulls you over for a taillight out, and he walks up to the window and sees someone who looks like Bob Marley wearing a T-shirt that says Legalize Marijuana across the front, and then he sees a *High Times* magazine lying open on the front seat, it would be another stupid human mistake to have marijuana anywhere near that car. The cop may or may not have probable cause to search the car, but I wouldn't bet the rent money on it. The police take the war on drugs seriously, and so should you. If you think maybe you would like to make a million dollars in the cannabis industry, you'd better understand the skills involved in transporting large amounts of marijuana. Going to prison over a plant will ruin your future as the entrepreneur of that new family business.

There are some simple rules of conduct that can help reduce the risk of being busted when you're transporting marijuana. If you look like a hippie, talk like a druggie, and drive when you're stoned, what do you think will happen if you get pulled over? Take the time to get a visual picture of what you're going to be doing with your life. An ounce is an ounce, and a pound is a pound, but the difference is measured in years when you're inside a courtroom. And when there are hundreds of pounds involved, which is what it will take to make a million dollars, your future could be bright or very gloomy, depending on the choices you make.

Transporting a pound of pot isn't that difficult, if you think about it. You should always keep the buds in the trunk, never in the cab, of the car. Eliminate as much of the smell as possible by squeezing out the air from the bag and double-bagging with ziplock bags (a Seal-a-Meal bag works great). Place the pound in a box and wrap it like a birthday present, complete with ribbon and card. Some people pour coffee grounds in the box to help with the smell. Put the gift box in a bag with perhaps several other gift boxes, and drive responsibly. If you get pulled over, try to relax, and don't act nervous. Have your car registration and proof of insurance all in one place, so you aren't fumbling around trying to find it. And don't drive without your license. Use "yes sir" and "no sir" a lot, and be respectful. If you drive a pickup or an SUV, keep your package in a locked tool box or an ice chest in the back of the vehicle. The difference between getting caught with an ounce or a pound is huge. Don't take my word for it; educate yourself.

Kilo Joe

By Chuck Allen Jr.

Back in the '70s, it was understood,
We bought our pot wherever we could.
My friends and I, if you really must know,
Bought our buds from Kilo Joe.

His name was Joe, from north Mexico.
His family grew buds south of San Diego.
He worked in a restaurant to cover his ass,
In case a policeman decided to ask.

They almost caught him in '72,
But he saw them coming and away he flew.
Returned to the States in '75,
Selling his kilos to stay alive.

Big droopy mustache down to his chin,
Big pearly teeth in the middle of a grin,
With buds in the back of a semitruck,
Covered with sand, just for luck.

Kilo Joe was a hell of a man,
Who sold his buds from a taco stand.
A kilo of buds under the beans;
Lunch on the corner is not what it seems.

The local policeman was never that wise;
Joe was selling pot right under his eyes.
Could only speak English from the third or fourth grade;
By the time he was thirty a million he'd made.

Joe raised a family and sent them to school;
Liberal Arts is the new golden rule.
His mustache is gray to match is hair;
He still sells his pot without a care.

I'll always remember that Mexican man,
Trying his best from a taco stand.
Selling his pot with a big ole' smile;
The American dream is all worthwhile.

CHAPTER 4

Secrets of a First-Time Grow

It's a two-mile hike up a sandy creek bed;
Take the fork to the left, and go straight ahead.

Before I begin this story, one that will motivate you one way or the other about your future in the cannabis industry, I just want to say this: there are good and bad people in all walks of life. There are good and bad lawyers, judges, doctors, surgeons, and marijuana growers. It's up to you to educate yourself, no matter what you're doing in life, but this is especially true in the cannabis industry. But if you take responsibility for your own actions and place your principles and values above everything else, then you'll be successful in whatever business you decide to start. Being an entrepreneur means that you may have to take many chances, and you have to be willing to fail, possibly many times. It means that you have to create the courage and confidence to push deeper into territories where you have never been before and realize that you could be all alone in the wilderness with no one else there to ask for help. You have to love without question what you are doing, because if you don't, everything else in your life will crumble like cornbread in cold buttermilk.

So my advice is to keep your new business venture to yourself, get your own place, and start small, until you gain some confidence in what you're doing. Maybe you can drop a few bags down in the woods or plant something exciting in your vegetable garden in the backyard. Next, move to a bigger house, and do something larger in the basement or garage. After that, move to the country, get completely off the grid, and try something that will positively change your life forever. All the while, keep looking for someone you can trust besides yourself—because somewhere along the line you're going to need a partner. It's dangerous to be in the woods alone. It's dangerous to sell large quantities of pot by yourself. There are bad people out there, and that's a hard lesson to learn by yourself— it could be your last. Remember this: *value* is always the price that you are willing to pay for something, and your *principles* are the agreements that you make with yourself.

In the fall of 1987, I went through a nasty divorce. I was making one mistake after another, and the more I tried to correct my situation the worst the mistakes became. I could see my life crumbling around me, and there was nothing I could do about. It was a very dark and depressing time in my life; even to this day I find it difficult to describe. I married a nineteen-year-old woman when I was thirty-seven. Let's just say I learned my lesson about young women, but it took four years and losing my son to realize that it takes more than good intentions to make a relationship work. I was managing restaurants and working sixty hours a week, and on a Saturday night, when I came home from a week of stress and frustration, exhausted beyond belief, she wanted to go dancing. She didn't understand what I was doing for a living, and I didn't understand why she was living with me. The chasm grew too wide and too deep for us to build a bridge, and one day we found ourselves standing on opposite sides of the Grand Canyon.

We had just bought a new house and car, and our son turned two years old, when one day over coffee, she dropped the bomb. She told me that the reason she had married me was to get away from her parents and ex-boyfriend, and she realized now what a big mistake she had made. She moved back to her parents, then back to me, then back to her parents, then back to me. By this time I was looking at a two-thousand-foot drop into hell. The last time she left was twenty-four years ago, and I haven't seen or heard from her or my son since. The most interesting thing about this time in my life was that I really did try to make things work. I quit drinking and smoking for over five years, working my fingers to the bone, and in the end none of my good intentions really mattered.

During this time I lost my job, which created more turmoil in my life, and things really started to spin out of control. I walked into my office at the restaurant one morning and found cocaine residue on my desk. It could only have been my assistant manager from the night before, so I started paying closer attention to his behavior, and I eventually caught him stealing money from the cash register. I followed procedures and went through the chain of command by reporting the problem to my district manager. Turns out the district manager had hired his nephew (which was against company policy) to work for me, so to solve the problem he fired me and promoted his nephew to take my job. (This gets back to that good guy/bad guy thing I was telling you about earlier.) At this point my life I had reached rock bottom, and I didn't know what I was going to do next. I had no family or friends living in the area, and I tried to look for work, but my heart wasn't in it.

I'm sure by now you're wondering what this has to do with making a million dollars in the cannabis industry, and to tell you the truth, I'm not sure I can explain the connection myself. I just know for a fact that I was willing to change my life completely only because the way I was living wasn't working for me. I didn't know that I was going to be growing pot in the woods and trying make a lot of money in the next few months. The thought didn't cross my mind, because for the past five years I had not taken one puff and hadn't really missed it that much. I think it's because, for me, marijuana exacerbates stressful situations, and the last thing I needed was to turn another thing I loved into a bad experience.

One night, before my phone was disconnected, I received a call from my ole' high-school buddy Don. He just happened to call to find out how I was doing, and of course I dumped my soap opera all over his head. Without hesitation, he invited me to come stay with him and his family until I could get back on my feet. Long story short, I packed what few belongings I had and drove to a small town in northern California. My home, until I found a job, was an air mattress inside a tent inside an unfinished garage, which Don was in the process of converting into a master bedroom.

It had been eight years since I'd seen Don, and at that time he had been scraping out a living as a handyman, finding work wherever he could. His drinking and smoking had been out of control, and he had been a bully to his family and friends. Because I had kicked his ass several times in the past, he had tended to leave me alone. Now I found him living in a four-bedroom home on five acres, with a swimming pool. He had four kids, one dog, three cats, two new cars, and a pickup truck. And if that wasn't enough, he and his wife had a housekeeper who was also the babysitter. I had known Don for over twenty years, and not once had he ever shown the ability or the desire to transform his life into more than just being a carpenter. Something was going on, but so far he wasn't willing to talk about it.

I lived in that tent for a month—with the dog, the ticks, and the fleas—until I found a bartender job and was able to save enough money to rent my own apartment. I was grateful for their hospitality and appreciated the opportunity, but Don was gone a lot and I never had the chance to talk to him about what was going on. One afternoon I asked his wife what he was doing for a living, and she mumbled something about him being a "business consultant." But that didn't make any sense, because Don was the last person anyone would pay for business advice because his own life had been so screwed up.

I loved my new bartending job; it was in a restaurant high on a bluff with a sweeping panoramic view. I was primarily the day bartender, but I also worked banquets and parties when needed. Attached to the lounge was a huge solarium that ran the length of the building, with plenty of sunshine to greet the customers. I got to meet wealthy and well-educated customers from all over the world, and my skills with the blender and knowledge of mixing drinks made me popular with employees and locals as well.

After I'd been working for a few months, my face became familiar to the locals, and they began to warm to my charm behind the bar. It's hard to keep a secret in a small community, especially where rumors and gossip are a way of life, and it didn't take long for the locals to start testing me with questions like, "You're Don's brother aren't you? What brings you to this town? How long do you plan on staying?" After they heard the answers they were looking for, they began to ask the real questions they wanted to ask, "Hey, man. Don's a good friend of mine. Know where I can get some coke?" "Dude, got any sugar?" "Say, man, got any Zig-Zags? I left mine at home." "Know where I can find some buds?" You didn't have to be a brain surgeon to figure out what was going on, but after all this time Don still hadn't told me what he was doing to support his family.

From time to time I was invited to Don's house for dinner, and we would sit around the glass dining room table and act like the normal American family. I couldn't seem to find the right moment to ask him about what was going on, and he seemed content on keeping me in the dark. I knew that small towns were notorious for making liars out of preachers and whores and it was just a matter of time before the truth came out.

The turning point came when Don promised his kids a weekend trip to Disneyland, and he asked me if I would be willing to stay at his house and feed the animals while they were gone. He gave me the key and asked that I keep the house locked at all times and be sure to spend the night because there had been some break-ins in the area, and he wanted to be sure nothing happened while they were away. I told him not to worry; it was the least I could do for all his hospitality.

The first night they were gone, I decided to do my laundry and accidentally found the cocaine in their laundry hamper. It was in a large plastic bag, on top of a scale, hidden under some dirty towels. I just about crapped my pants. I don't do cocaine, never have done cocaine, but I can tell you one thing for sure: I know what it looks like when I see it. It looks like a long walk off a short pier, and I made sure all my fingerprints were wiped clean before I put it back.

I may have done the Tiburon shuffle a few hundred times, but to me there was a clear line between marijuana and cocaine, and somewhere deep inside I still had principles and values that knew the difference. I felt terrible about what Don was doing with his life and his family; his integrity was hanging out there so far he couldn't see it with a telescope.

I hadn't smoked a joint in almost six years, and I sure felt I could use one now. Maybe a puff or two and a good movie would help me forget that my long time friend was dealing cocaine with his wife kids in the house. So I said to myself, *Fuck it! If there's pot in the house, I'm going to find it.* I started to search. I looked in all the usual places: night stand, dresser drawers, bookshelves, behind picture frames, in the refrigerator, in the freezer, but then bingo-bango, I found it in the coffee can in the kitchen pantry. I didn't know whether the pot belonged to Don, his wife, or the housekeeper, but it was obvious that whoever made the coffee in the morning knew it was there. I made a pipe out of a cardboard paper-towel roll and relaxed in front of the VCR, watching *Ferris Beuller's Day Off.*

The next morning was my day off, and after breakfast I took the dog for a walk around the property. In back of the old barn was a fenced-in garden about the size of a two-car garage, and over in one corner was a homemade greenhouse made of two-by-fours and sheets of plastic. I'd always liked greenhouses, and this was a good one. Then, much to my surprise, I found a dried-up marijuana leaf on the ground that looked as if it had been dropped a few weeks ago. It was late October, and most of the garden had already been picked clean, except for some cabbage and squash scattered around here and there. Outside the garden fence was a large pile of green garden hose stacked near a water faucet. I guessed there was at least six hundred feet of coiled hose. At first I didn't think so much about it, but then I wondered why so much hose was piled beside a garden that was only a few feet away. That's when I saw the dog disappear into the bushes, and when I took a closer look, I could see a well-worn path leading into the manzanita trees. The dog was a very large German shepherd, very friendly, very goofy, and very easy to follow. When I came to a small clearing where I was able to straighten up, I found ten female pot plants, each standing twelve feet tall, in full bloom and ready to harvest. It was the first time in my life I had seen cannabis plants growing in the wild. I remember thinking to myself, *These plants are the most beautiful girls I've ever seen.* The midmorning sunlight was filtering through the branches, casting a kaleidoscope of colors around the shoulders of the ladies in waiting.

They stood there tempting me with the fruits of their desire. I could smell their calling and taste their wild purpose of intentions. I crossed my legs and sat down on the ground, stunned with the silence and wonder. of it all. I was mentally gulping for oxygen, trying to gain balance on the edge of adventure. Deep in the solar plexus of my spirit, I had to make this plant my venture to success, my frolic with enterprise, and the destiny of my expedition in life.

Drifuss the dog, was acting as if he wanted me to keep following him farther along the trail. Stooping and crawling between the trees and underbrush, I came to another garden, and then another—until

I had found eighty plants scattered around the property. My friend Don, knowing full well that I was a lover of the magical herb, had deliberately chosen not to share with me the part of his life that I found most interesting.

Now I knew what all that garden hose was for. The plants were cleverly hidden, but they needed water. I admired the camouflage and all the hard work it must have taken to create such a beautiful secret garden.

I took the dog back to the house and gave him water and food. What a good boy for leading me to Don's secret garden! I returned to the garden with a ziplock bag and scissors, where I carefully harvested enough buds to last me well into the holidays and probably into next year. I made sure to take some dirt and rub it into the freshly cut stems so the missing buds wouldn't be noticed.

I drove back to my place and put the buds in a paper bag so they could slowly dry out in a cool room. By the time Don and the family returned from their trip, I had a big fat bag of some fresh Humbolt Skunk buds, and I was as happy as a thief could possibly get. As much as I disliked Don, there was something about his gardening skills that I admired, and I wanted to learn more. I had this burning desire to find out what it took to grow large amounts of marijuana buds and to be successful doing it.

I didn't know exactly how to approach Don about the cocaine, and I certainly wasn't going to bring up the subject of his hidden garden around the house, so I decided to let everything evaporate somewhere in the corner of my regret. Things have a way of working themselves out, given enough time. But Don had his own karma to work out, and hopefully it wouldn't be inside some prison cell somewhere. It certainly wasn't my intention to be involved with cocaine or people who are stupid enough to sell it in a small town. That's one stupid human mistake I'll let someone else deal with.

A few days before Christmas, I went to Don's house to give presents to the family for the holidays. I asked how the remodeling was going in the garage, and he couldn't wait to show me his handiwork. The new bedroom was complete except for the furniture and the light fixture on the ceiling. The east and west walls had walk-in closets with full-length mirrored doors that gave the room a sense of expansion. The north wall had no windows, because it faced the driveway and carport. The south wall was a solid closure of windows and sliding glass doors that overlooked the swimming pool and the horizon beyond. The entire room was filled with reflective sunlight; it was very bright and very cheery. I was definitely impressed with Don's carpentry skills. As we took a seat on the new carpet and made ourselves comfortable, I couldn't help thinking how far he had come since the last time I had seen him eight years ago.

He asked me how things were going at the restaurant, and before I knew it, the words just jumped out of my mouth. I told him that people were coming up to me at the bar asking for drugs because they thought I was his brother, and I asked him what was going on. He looked at me with an expression that said, "Okay, you caught me. I wasn't going to tell you, but now I guess I better." Over the next two hours, he told me what had happened when we'd both left Tiburon in 1980.

Don had married and moved to northern California, while I had married and moved to Oregon. All his adult life he had been a mean, nasty drunk who took out his anger and bitterness on the people closest him. One night he had been driving home from a night of alcohol and drug abuse when he drove off the road, and the only thing that saved him from a two-hundred-foot fall into canyon was a small pine tree about the size of a flagpole. He told me how he had gotten out of the truck and fallen down on his knees and promised the Lord that he would never do drugs again, and he assured me he hadn't. He'd stayed in the construction business, but the work hadn't been steady enough to help him raise his growing family, so they'd taken a loan from his wife's mother and opened a restaurant. He found out too late that he didn't have the experience for such a lofty dream, and he started selling cocaine to help pay the bills that were mounting up on a daily basis. The restaurant was a losing proposition almost from the start, and it finally began to show signs of sinking after the second winter.

Don had met a customer who was a crooked cop, from Oakland. He stole pounds of cocaine from the evidence room and "fronted" it to Don, who then would "front" ounces to his friends, who then would sell grams to the local workers in town. When Don collected enough money to pay for the drugs, he would return to Oakland and pick up another pound. This went on for several years, until problems with the locals not showing up for work, rent not being paid, and people getting hooked started to come to the attention of the community leaders. Don was very popular with his employees and many of the locals, but he couldn't keep the restaurant doors open. In order to pay off his creditors, he had to keep dealing, and in that process his wife got hooked, and she used the drug for social networking with neighbors and friends. He sold the restaurant and managed to pay off the bulk of his debt. The cocaine that he had left was the last of that business venture. He was helping his wife deal with her drug addiction, but it wasn't easy.

He had made enough money to pay for their house and property but not enough to pay for the taxes. He started to exchange grams of coke for remodeling work on the house, and then cash flow problems doubled and tripled, and then the crooked cop showed up looking for his money, and that's when things turned ugly. It was at that point that a friend of his got him into growing pot. He used cocaine to buy into a partnership for a major grow that they had done the previous summer, and within four months he had made a quarter of a million dollars and paid off all his debts. Now they were just dealing with his wife's addiction.

He said that he had been growing small gardens for the past six years, but last year he had learned a lot from the biggest pot grower in northern California. He wanted to do one more big grow and then sell the house and move to another state where the weather wasn't so foggy and damp. Even though he doesn't smoke marijuana anymore, he still can't get over that spiritual feeling he gets every time he walks into a secret garden. There's something honest and straightforward about growing cannabis that no one is willing to talk about—which is okay, because the money that's being generated in the industry is quietly being spent in the economy to help this country survive the political war on drugs that was started by the Progressive movement over seventy years ago. His friend the entrepreneur had made millions in the cannabis industry and used it to buy a supermarket, a gas station, gift shops, and two bed-and-breakfast inns in the area. Americans don't care how you make your money; they only care that you have the money. It's the government and the IRS who want to control how you make your money.

I told Don about the Tiburon shuffle and all the interesting characters that I had met along the way. I described how I had not made a lot of money but did have a good time until I got married and screwed everything up. After a while I'd realized that I was on the wrong end of the business, and what I really wanted to do was be the farmer, not the broker. Don advised that marriage also took work, but growing pot in the woods was the hardest work he had ever done in his life, and the most dangerous too. His last partner had been sixty-seven years old and a master at growing pot in the woods, but he should have given it up years ago. One day it started to rain on their way out of the wilderness, and the old man slipped on a rock and twisted his ankle really badly. Don had to carry him almost three miles back to safety, and it was on that struggle back to civilization that he realized that his partner would not have been able to carry him if he had twisted his ankle. There was not just the risk of losing the crop to forest fires and deer; there was the risk of losing your life to falling trees and rattlesnakes. Anything could go wrong in the woods and usually did, somewhere along the way.

The average pot smoker, sitting at home playing video games and listening to music, didn't think about how the pot was grown or who the farmer was. He was just glad someone did it and it wasn't him. He probably thought it had something to do with the Mexican drug cartel or the Chicago mafia, never realizing that the American cannabis industry was made up of independent entrepreneurs who had decided to rule themselves.

As we sat there on the new carpet, telling stories about what had happened over the past few years, Don started talking about a friend of his who had moved to Hawaii and retired from the pot-farming business. Don knew where the old grow site was and wondered whether I would be interested in being his partner. Of course I agreed, and we began to make plans to work the site in the spring. This was the opportunity that I had been looking for. I had found a mentor that I could trust and who could trust me. If we didn't kill each other, maybe I could learn a new trade and make some serious money along the way.

The deal was made: since this was my first grow, and I had no money, we would divide the sale with 60 percent for him and 40 percent for me. For every ten pounds of dried buds, he would get six and I would get four. His reason was because it was his site, his tools, his seeds, and his experience, and the agreement seemed reasonable to me. He suggested that I stop smoking and start running on the beach to get in shape, because I was about to become a guerrilla farmer in the wilderness of northern California!

In the second week of April, when the weather permitted, we went to the grow site to see how much work was needed to get the garden ready for planting. I had my new hiking boots on, a backpack with sandwiches, and two bottles of water. I converted an old mop handle into a walking stick with a rubber tip. It would take us two hours to hike in and two hours to hike out; that left four hours of daylight to get some work done. Don's wife would be the taxi; she would drive us twenty-three miles into the countryside to drop us off at the rendezvous spot and pick us up eight hours later. We couldn't park in the area, because the locals would wonder why a car was parked on the side of the road and become suspicious that someone might be trespassing on their property. The whole idea was not to arouse suspicion!

The spot where we started our hike was in between two farmhouses that were about two hundred yards apart. We had to be careful, because dogs could hear our footsteps from a long way off and think we were deer; once again, the idea was not to arouse suspicion. From the road we walked down the hill, using the trees and brush as cover until we reached the creek. Then we turned west toward the wooded hills in the distance. In the spring the creek had a steady flow of water, but in August it dried up to a trickling stream, with only a few deep pools along its course. One of the first lessons I learned was how to walk to and from a grow site without leaving a trail. That meant no footprints, no skid marks, no trash, no smoking, no noise—no evidence of any kind that someone had passed in that direction. It's a real tough skill that you have to practice in order to be good at.

About a mile into the hike, the creek branched to the right; we stayed to the left. After another half mile, the creek hit a rock bank and split in half; we stayed to the left. Another half mile, and the creek started a steep climb up the hill, with rocks and boulders forming a crude stairway. (This is a great place for rattlesnakes and a constant reminder that with every step danger could be lurking in the shadows of those crevices.) The entrance to the hidden grow site was on the right side of the creek, up the bank, about twenty feet away, and at a crucial place where absolutely no evidence or signs showed that anyone had climbed out of the creek and entered the garden. We took off our boots and climbed on the rocks, up the bank, to the corner of a fence line where a small gate to the garden had been made. Once we were inside, we put our boots back on and began our inspection. The grow site was much bigger than I had expected. The fence line was made from plastic bird netting that ran the perimeter of the garden and divided the site in half, forming two separate gardens on the west side of a steep hillside.

The first thing that we noticed was that the fence line needed to be replaced because of the damage caused by deer, wild pigs, raccoons, skunks, rabbits, cougar, bear, and any number of critters that could have been roaming their forest domain. We made fences by using the bird netting, which come in 7' x 20' packages, which made it easy to carry in our backpacks. The idea was to stretch cord or fishing line from tree to tree around the perimeter of the garden and tie it about six feet off the ground. Then we attached the bird netting to the cord with twist ties as we moved down the line, stretching the netting tight until the fence was upright and stable. It was important to create a "gate" that would allow easy access to each garden but still keep the critters out. This garden had three gates. Once the fence was up, we needed to secure the bottom of the netting with rocks, tree limbs, logs, etc. to help keep smaller critters from getting under the fence. The truth is, fences don't keep determined animals out, but they help to discourage them from coming in, and the farmer needs all the help he can get! It's also good to remember that in the event that the garden does get busted, everything you do out there is an additional felony. (Rat traps, mouse traps, ant traps, insect spray, bug repellant, and bird netting are all considered dangers to wildlife if found in a pot garden, but they are perfectly all right if found in your garden at home. Thought I would mention that just for fun.)

Next we checked the water lines, which seemed to be in fairly good shape; only the filters needed to be cleaned and changed. Water lines are more important than fence lines, because without water there would be no garden. It's crucial to understand that water lines take skill, knowledge, and a tremendous amount of labor to install correctly. A good water line is the heartbeat of the garden, just as a good cook is the heartbeat of a restaurant; they both need to be employed with respect and consideration. Sometimes it takes the entire summer to install water and fence lines and dig holes for planting in the year to come. (That piece of information alone is worth a million dollars.) With water lines, the idea is to let gravity do all the work. Make sure that your water source (creek, spring, pond, lake, etc.) will be there in late August, because it would be a shame to watch your plants die of thirst after so much hard work. (Avoiding that stupid human mistake is worth another million dollars.) You'll need to buy flexible PVC pipe, both one inch and two inch, with spaghetti line, emitters, connectors, T-connecters, elbows, reducers, and PVC glue. Estimating how much equipment you'll need is another skill that you'll have to learn by doing. Remember to use only cash; don't leave a paper trail.

It's also a good idea not to leave paper or plastic bags with cash register receipts, or any item that has a bar code on it, anywhere near the grow site. People have gone to jail because they left candy wrappers in their gardens.

Two of the most important items you can buy for your garden are battery-operated timers and filter screens for the water lines. Timers will save you from hours of hiking out to the garden and back just to water the plants. You set the timer to come on for an hour in the morning and for an hour in the afternoon, and you'll only have to go to the garden once every two weeks. The screens will filter the pipes for frogs and polliwogs and contain them to one area for easy cleaning.

When you get ready to install the watering system, lay out the pipes in the general direction that you want the water to flow all the way to the entrance gate, making sure you have enough sections to cover the garden. PVC pipe usually come in fifty—to a hundred-foot rolls; they aren't heavy but they're kind of bulky, and carrying even one roll two miles into the woods can be a challenge. Two people carrying one hundred feet of pipe will take three trips just for six hundred feet of water line. (That's three days of hiking just with pipe! And if you happen to need twelve hundred feet, that's a lot of work just to get water pipe to the grow site—and it's not even installed yet.)

You'll probably want to use two-inch pipe at the water source and then reduce it to one-inch pipe when you get to the garden site.

The end of the pipe that you're going to sink into the bottom of your water source will need to be covered with a screen to prevent rocks and dirt from being sucked into the pipe and clogging the line. Attach the screen to the pipe with wire or fishing line. The water we were using filled a pool that was spring fed from deep inside a mountain and never went dry. Our garden site had been picked because it had a forty-degree slant on the side of a hill, so that gravity would help the water flow down the hill easily. It was steep but not so difficult that we couldn't walk; we just had to be careful, because one slip and we could end up in the creek below. I bet you thought that growing pot in the woods was going to be easy, but it's complicated, hard work, and the dangers come from many different directions. For instance, a tick bite can bring with it something called Lyme disease, which is a very painful medical condition known to cause a lifetime of misery. Just digging a hole can uncover a handful of scorpions or an angry nest of wasps.

Once you have the water line all pieced together, attach the timers and install the filters (one by each gate). Reduce the two-inch line to a one-inch line, bring it under the fence into the garden, lay it vertically down the hillside, and then cap the end. Forgetting to buy end caps will cost you another day of hiking.

At this point you have a choice to make: are you going to dig holes or fill bags? Both are labor intensive, and both require you to notch out the side of the hill so the bags will stand up level. I like to dig the holes and plant directly in the ground, but a lot of farmers like the grow bags because they can be placed under and around trees more easily, without having to deal with roots and rocks. Keep in mind that sometimes, in hot weather, plastic bags will scorch the roots that grow too close to the outside of the bags, causing slow growth or poor bud production. If you're looking to make a lot of money, you need to dig a lot of holes or fill a lot of bags. There are many formulas and opinions out there concerning how many plants should be planted per hole or bag and the number of buds that can be produced. But the truth is that water, soil (nutrients), sun, seeds, temperature (shade), and what I call the X factor (insects, mice, birds, etc.), all play the biggest role in determining the health and productivity of the plants in each hole or bag.

Generally speaking, for six to eight seedlings, you would dig a hole two feet wide by three feet long and eighteen inches deep. Break up the soil, remove the rocks, add a cup of all-purpose fertilizer high in nitrogen, and mix well. Once you sex the plants and remove all the males, you can probably expect four or five female plants per hole (sometimes more, sometimes less, depending on genetics and the X factor). Anyway, four or five healthy mature female plants could be expected to produce eight to sixteen ounces per hole (four to eight ounces when dried). If you are going to use expensive commercial grow bags or store-bought large plastic garbage bags, expect to plant four to six seedlings per bag, with two to three female plants after sexing. Be aware that plastic reflects light and can be seen easily from the air. (What Don has done in the past is plant twelve to fifteen plants per hole and, after taking out the males, end up with six to ten females per hole.) The problem with over-bunching plants is the increased chance of mold due to poor air circulation, and the tendency for insects and disease to move from one plant to the next. So, there's something to the old adage Less is Better. After the holes are dug and the bags are filled, it's time to attach the spaghetti lines and emitters to the one-inch water lines and place them in the prepared soil.

One of the toughest problems you'll have with a garden that's remote is getting the water from the source to the garden site. It's almost never accomplished on the first try and often not on the first day. Sometimes it will take engineering skills you thought you never had. Remember, you'll need a six—to eight-foot drop (or more) in elevation to get enough pressure to start the water flowing inside the pipe. This is not an easy task to manage, especially if you're trying to bring the water up and over a creek bank or across a long flat stretch of ground with no incline. I'm sure there is a plumber's tool or some kind of device out there that doesn't require electricity that will do the job, but I haven't found it yet. Anyway, I usually go back to the water source and disconnect the first and second pipe and suck on the end as if I were siphoning gas from a car. When the water starts to flow, I move down the line and try to keep it moving. It's probably best that you don't glue the water pipe together until you have water flowing to the garden site. (That piece of information is worth a million bucks too.)

Now, let's stop for a moment and think about where we are. On paper, hiking through the woods, building a fence, designing a workable water system, and digging fifty to a hundred holes doesn't sound that difficult. But in reality, each one of those projects could take days, weeks, months, or even years to complete, depending on time, distance, weather, your physical condition, and finances. A person can only carry so many bags of fertilizer, tools, and supplies—not to mention, food, water, medical supplies, and various weapons you might need to protect yourself while you're in the wilderness.

I bet you thought that growing pot in the woods was going to be easy, but it's just about as easy as climbing a mountain; you'd better know what you're doing, or you could get yourself killed. It's very bad to get halfway up the side of a four-thousand-foot mountain and quit because you're too scared to continue. It's just as dangerous to go down as it is to go up, and it takes the same number of balls to continue either way.

Those early pioneers who found the courage and determination to cross rivers, mountains, and deserts to settle a hostile land were a different breed of human beings than the people who stayed back in their comfortable homes, content with life the way that it was. Today, those entrepreneurs that I like to call pioneer farmers have the same courage and determination it takes to cross a hostile political frontier and prove that man can still rule himself without the help of big government.

Let's do some math. Pretend that you and your partner planted a remote garden and harvested fifty pounds of fresh-cut buds. After four days of letting them dry, you start to weight them into one-pound ziplock bags and, much to your surprise, you discover that you now only have twenty-five pounds of buds that you can sell, because there was a 50 percent loss of moisture from the drying process. (Nobody wants to buy wet buds because they wouldn't be getting their money's worth.) Let's assume that the buds are top quality and have no seeds. The formula should look something like this, based on the current market price of $2,500 a pound.

25 lb. x $2,500 bulk rate = $62,500, divided by 2 = $31,250 tax-free income for each partner. Not bad pay for only four or five months' work, but it's a far cry from a million dollars. Factor in your cost for gas, supplies, labor, and other expenses, and your profit is reduced considerably. So, let's scratch out some more numbers, just to see exactly what it would take to make a million dollars growing pot in the woods. If at the end of the season you harvested 400 pounds and packaged 200 one-pound bags of dried product, the formula would look something like this:

200 lb. x $2,500 bulk rate = $500,000, divided by 2 = $250,000 tax-free income for each partner. Stands to reason that you would have to double your production to make a million dollars. That means you would have to grow 800 pounds of buds to get 400 pounds of dried product at the end of the season.

The formula for making a million dollars should look something like this:

400 lb. x $2,500 bulk rate = $1 million divided by 2 = $500,000 tax-free income for each partner. This is the yardstick you're looking for—this is the key. 400 lb. x $2,500 = $1 million tax-free.

Assuming that you could get your hands on 400 pounds of dried marijuana buds, how would you sell it? Just exactly who would buy it? What are you going to do, walk up to the college dean and ask him if he has any buyers? Have you ever thought about how much time it would take to dig 800 holes (assuming you could harvest one pound per hole)? Food for thought! I'll let that idea sink in for a while; in the meantime, let's get back to Don's gardening class in the woods.

As Don and I walked around the old grow site on the side of the hill, we determined that the fence could be repaired easily and the water line was in good shape except for new timers and filters. There were 200 holes, counting both gardens, but they needed a lot of work. If we each worked on fifteen holes a day, we could have them cleared and fertilized in about a week (if we hiked out there every day). Just for practice, go out in the woods and try digging one two-foot by three-foot by eighteen-inch-deep hole in half an hour.

Then try digging two holes in one hour, or eight holes in four hours; take a break for lunch, and then dig seven more holes. You'd better be in shape, because you've got to do the same thing again for the next six days!

We divided fertilizer into five-pound bags and carried two at a time in our backpacks. Timers, batteries, emitters, and spaghetti line we could also carry in the backpacks. We would need two pickaxes, two shovels, and a hand saw for cutting branches and small trees (and probably a forty-pound dig bar for digging rocks and hard ground). It would take three or four trips just to bring in those supplies.

We needed some kind of a handgun stashed in a plastic bag somewhere inside the garden, in case of emergencies. I know this is the twenty-first century, but there are dangers in the woods (rattlesnakes are the first to come to mind). I was surrounded by a pack of wild dogs once, and all I had was a tree branch to fight them off with, and it wasn't easy. I could have very easily been killed or seriously injured if they hadn't been more interested in the deer they were chasing. A handgun wouldn't help much with a bear or a wild hog, but it's better than nothing.

For those of you who don't like handguns, you'd better think twice about growing pot in the woods. If you discover a rattlesnake in your garden, or if she discovers you, there will be more terror in your peaceful garden than you could possibly imagine, because the whole mountain is her home and she isn't going away quietly, especially if she has babies. And don't be foolish enough to try coaxing the snake away with sticks and tree limbs, because if you make one mistake, it could be your last. Think about this for a moment: if you were bitten and you were as remote as we were, it would be a two-hour walk to the nearest county road, and then you would have to flag down a vehicle and ask them to drive you to the nearest hospital, twenty-three miles away. It's true that you might not die, but it's equally true that you might not live, either—all because of your strongly held opinions about guns. Could be your strongly held opinions will get you killed. Which is more important—you kill the snake or the snake kills you?

If it's against your principles to kill any living thing, then don't grow a garden in the woods. If you don't kill the ants, grasshoppers, crickets, mice, rats, or any other number of critters, then they will kill your crop, and that defeats your purpose for being in the woods in the first place.

After the garden site is ready for planting, you'll need to go back and bury the water lines or camouflage them with rocks, dirt, tree limbs, and leaves, etc. PVC pipe can be seen from the air, and people walking in the woods might come across it, follow it back to your garden, and bingo-bango, the party is over. Once you have the water lines camouflaged, you'll need to start thinking about planting your nursery bed for seedlings. Fortunately for us, we were using seeds from Don's past grows. We had tens of thousands of hybrid Skunk Bud seeds (*sativa* 60 percent and *indica* 40 percent). And we were fortunate that we didn't have to worry about seed stock—that part of the business is too important to leave to happenstance. A considerable amount of money and thought needs to be devoted to this area, because poor-quality seeds will produce poor-quality plants. It's one of the most common mistakes neophytes make when starting a garden, not knowing where the seeds came from. Even good seeds mixed with different strains of good seeds will produce a crop that is mixed, with various shades of color, and it may not bring the top price that growers are looking for. If you're trying to make a million dollars selling 400 pounds of dried buds to a professional buyer, he'll be looking for consistency in the color and the quality of the smoke. He's looking to make sure all the buds are the same color, smell, shape, and density. He'll also test the quality of the smoke to see if it's the best on the market. Sometimes the quality of the smoke is better than the color indicates, but that's an exception, not the rule.

Using the formula of 400 pounds of dried buds x $2,500 bulk rate price = $ million tax-free, you'll need to find at least 1,600 top-quality seeds. Half of them will be males, and water evaporation will necessitate 400 female plants for your final product.

It's a sad lesson when you go through all that hard work and only make a thousand dollars a pound because the seeds you were using were of poor quality. And on top of your disappointment, the buyer will be reluctant to come back to you again because his customers are looking for the best quality smoke he can find, and you failed to deliver. That piece of advice is worth a million dollars. Anyway, it's a catch-22 situation for some first-time growers, because if they don't have the money to buy top-quality seeds, then they are forced to use whatever seeds they have on hand, and if the crop comes in seeded, then those seeds are poor quality, and the wheel goes around and around. But if the farmer is smart, he'll use some of his profit and buy top-quality seeds for his next grow.

There are many seed companies that will sell you top-quality seeds at anywhere from a dollar to twenty dollars or more per seed, depending on the quality you're looking for. Seeds are a global business these days; all you have to do is go on the Internet or buy a marijuana magazine and you'll find every variety of pot seed known to the free marketplace. (Marijuana magazines and books are also a global industry.) Of course, the United States and her partners in crime have made marijuana seeds illegal to possess, purchase, import, or export on the free market, so be smart about what you're doing. Never buy seeds with a check or credit card, and never have seeds sent to the address where your garden is located. The best and safest way to get top-quality seeds is to purchase a ten pack of the best seeds you can find for around a hundred dollars from a good seed company (have the seeds sent to a friend's house), and do a closet grow yourself, allowing one or two males to pollinate the female plants. You'll get thousands of fresh seeds when you harvest. Those are the seeds you'll want to plant in the woods for a million-dollar crop.

Anyway, back to Don's school of gardening in the wilderness. The seeds that we were using came from his last grow which became "seeded" when they over looked one or two male plants. (which is easy to do when you consider there are hundreds perhaps thousands of plants in one garden). They didn't get the price they were looking for but on the other hand, they got enough seeds to last them a life time. Don claims to have sold a gallon jar full of Skunk seeds to a Mexican friend for $40,000, could it have been the same waiter friend of mine from Tiburon and the singing American black man from Mexico? That's one of those "don't ask don't tell" situations I mentioned before, it's best to just listen and learn. One of the reasons my percentage of the harvest was only 40 percent was because I had no seeds to bring to the table. Never underestimate the value of a marijuana seed, Napoleon started a war over the hempseed and so did the US government. Funny how we never learn from history. Our founding fathers knew the value of the hempseed, in fact our first twenty-nine presidents didn't have a problem with the hemp industry until the progressive movement found a way to collapse the free enterprise system. Don't take my word for it, look it up for yourself. It's important for you to have a good reason to take your country back or at least stand on your own two feet and learn how to rule yourself. The idea of "one man one vote" may be in danger of being destroyed but there's only one industry still alive today that can save the American people and that's the cannabis industry.

There are some guerrilla farmers who plant their pot seeds in a greenhouse or start their seedlings under fluorescent lights and then carry them out to the garden site in the woods. To me it's a cumbersome and time-consuming task, especially if the hike is several miles into the wilderness. Packing and unpacking small plants puts needless stress on baby plants. The best way to plant your secret garden is to make your own greenhouse in the woods and start your seeds near the grow site. Wait until the fear of frost is gone (usually the second week of May), and then prepare an area inside the fence about the size of a dining room rug, ten feet by six feet, turning the soil and clearing it as you would for a flowerbed.

Scatter twenty pounds of potting soil mix over the area and work it into the soil until the ground is smooth and soft. Then sow the seeds evenly over the area and cover them with a thin layer of potting soil mix, making sure the seeds are not covered by more than a half inch. Sprinkle water on the soil, making sure the seeds are damp but not soaked. Take small logs and place them on the east and west side of the planting bed, stretch clear plastic sheets across the bed, and tuck the edges under the logs for support. Leave the ends open for air circulation. The plastic sheets should be no more than six inches from the top of the soil. Be sure to pick a sunny spot for the nursery.

Check the seeds every two or three days, making sure the soil doesn't dry out. When the sprouts have developed so that the stem emerges from the surface of the soil, you will notice two small seed leaves. If the empty seed case is still attached to the top of a stem, don't attempt to remove it, because a seedling is very delicate, and you may inadvertently damage it in the process. When the first true leaves have developed, the seedlings are ready to be transplanted into the hole or bag. We used a regular tablespoon to carefully scoop out the individual seedlings and carry them to their new home. It is a time-consuming process to plant that way, but it's better than backpacking eight hundred seedlings two miles into the wilderness! Give each baby plant a drink of water, making sure they are firmly standing on their own before placing the emitters near the plants and turning on the water. In the first two weeks of transplanting, the seedlings need to be checked as often as possible. When the plants are six inches tall, you can place a teaspoon of Rapid Grow fertilizer in front of each emitter once every two weeks. When the plants are eighteen inches tall, some farmers like to cut the tops off the plants to encourage them to grow out instead of up; this creates more branches and consequently more buds. The rule of thumb is "Knee high by the Fourth of July."

Once the garden is up and running by itself, you should only have to go out there once a week to check on timers, filters, water lines, fence line, insects, health of the plants, and generally look for any problems that you can find, especially signs of human visitors to the area (footprints, cigarette butts, candy wrappers, fresh shell casings etc.). You would be surprised at the number of people who are walking around deep in the woods. One of the biggest concerns for pot growers is deer season—which opens in late September and early October—because it's so close to harvest time.

One day Don and I were having lunch in the garden, and we could hear a truck approaching above us from a gravel road maybe a mile away. (Sound travels a long distance in the outdoors.) When the truck stopped, there was silence for a few minutes, and then we heard the voices of two men but couldn't make out the words. There was lots of whooping and hollering, as if they were really drunk or high or something and having a good time. Then there was more silence for about five minutes, and we thought the truck had moved on over the hill and gone away. So we were munching on our sandwiches and crunching on our corn chips when all of a sudden someone opened up with some kind of automatic rifle fire: *bruppa-brup-brup, bruppa-brup-brup*, and then another automatic weapon, *bruppa-brup-brup, bruppa-brup-brup*! Don and I dove for cover where there wasn't any. The way the sound was reverberating between the hills, it sounded as if the two guys were standing right below us in the creek bed. But we could hear the bullets snapping the tree limbs above our heads, and we knew they were standing on the hill in back of us, shooting down into the canyon. They were making us crap our pants. If they knew we were down there and they decided to follow the creek to find us, we were dead meat; it would be every man for himself.

Don grabbed the handgun and his backpack, I grabbed my backpack and the canteen, and we both dove under the fence, scrambled up the hill, and hid behind a large pine tree. Our plan was to take the fight to them and not wait for them to find us. We only had six bullets, but we intended to make each one count. By the time we were clear about what we were going to do, the shooting stopped, and we heard the truck drive away. We worried and debated about those two guys for a long time; even today we still don't know whether they knew we were only a few hundred yards down the hill from where they were standing. But there was one thing we did know for sure: trying to make a living growing pot in the middle of the woods was the last of the American adventures. If we weren't killed by rattlesnakes, wild bears, or stray bullets, we were destined to become millionaires.

Most pot farmers mark their planting date on a calendar so they can keep track of the number of days until harvest. It takes about 120 days, give or take a week. Even the most experienced growers sometimes disagree on when's the right time, especially if one of them doesn't smoke, which is what happened between Don and me. He wanted to wait another week, and I said it was time to harvest, because I had already tasted the product. So, we harvested half the crop and came back a week later and got the rest. Turned out either way was fine.

If you're standing in your garden trying to decide when to harvest, here's what you do. Take a close look at the bud and you will see slender white appendages, or fibers, on the buds; these are called pistils. Simply put, they are the ovaries of the seed plant. When pollen from a male cannabis plant floats on the wind and lands on that part of the female cannabis plant, she will produce seeds. This is not a good thing if you're looking for top price for your harvest, because consumers don't like smoking seeds; it takes away from the flavor and aroma of the smoke. But it's a good thing if the farmer is looking to replenish his seed stock. As a rule of thumb, when about 70 percent of the pistils on the bud have turned from white to red or light brown in color, the buds are ready to harvest. There are more precise indicators amongst some growers, but microscopes and jewelers' loupes aren't usually found in the woods.

Once we decided it was time to harvest, we had two options: harvest the whole plant or just the buds. Since we were two miles from our vehicle, harvesting only the buds was the best choice. But I still hated to see all those leaves go to waste, because there was so much they could have been used for (cookies, brownies, marijuana butter, and hash, to name a few). We harvested the buds from the tops of the plants first (because they receive the most sunlight and mature the fastest), and then we came back and harvested the rest of the crop a few days later. The hike back to the county road to catch our "taxi" was a lot harder than I'd imagined. We each carried two plastic bags weighing twenty-five pounds, a piece, plus our backpacks, making each step of the way difficult; it was practically impossible not to leave tracks along the creek bed. Carrying two awkward bags slung over the shoulders and trying not to twist an ankle or step on a snake isn't something the average person goes out and trains for. After the first mile, my arms felt like rubber bands, and the last two hundred yards, coming out of the creek, just about killed me. But I kept saying to myself, *Money does grow on trees. Money does grow on trees*, all the way to the top of the hill.

By the time we reached the county road, the smell of the fresh-cut buds had penetrated our clothes, hair, and skin; we smelled like two dead skunks on the side of the road. When our taxi arrived, we tossed the four bags into the trunk and covered them with a plastic tarp. Thank goodness Don had done this before and knew exactly what to do. We took our clothes off, including our shoes and socks, put them in double plastic bags, and covered them with blankets on the back floorboards. We took rubbing alcohol and washed our skin as best we could; then we got dressed in clean jeans, sweatshirts, and flip-flops. We rolled down the windows and used air freshener to help clear the funky air. Don's wife lit up a cigarette, and that helped cover the smell too. The chances of us being pulled over were slim, but you never knew on those backwoods country roads. All we had to do was watch our speed and remain calm.

The good Lord was with us, and we made it back safely. All we had to do now was return to the garden in a few days and do the whole thing over again, which we did. After harvesting all the buds and collecting then in one place, we were ready for the drying stage of the business. Just to reach this phase of our goal was a great achievement, and we were exhausted. Six months of intense mental and physical labor had squeezed all the piss and vinegar out of us, and we needed some time to ourselves. But we still had two hundred pounds of fresh buds to dry, and we had to keep going.

The drying process is an art form and can make the difference between a smooth-tasting toke or a harsh, choking smoke. The difference is a longer and slower drying process in a cooler environment. A lot of farmers get in a hurry after harvesting, and they want to dry their crops as fast as they can so they can get the money and run. But the old pros know that's a mistake that will cost them money at the bargaining table. Fortunately for me, Don knew what he was doing and was in no hurry. His barn was completely set up with everything we needed. There were sawhorses with screen doors laid out neatly in rows of six, with four aisles in between. After removing the fan leaves (these could be dried and used in cooking, etc.) we laid out the buds evenly on the screens and allowed them to rest in a cool (60 to 75 degrees), dark place for four to seven days, or longer when humidity levels were below 50 percent. As long as there is air circulation around the buds, there's no need to turn them over. You just keep a sharp eye out for mold, which means that there is too much moisture in the room and you need to get some warm, dry air flowing in a hurry by turning on some fans. Two hundred pounds of freshly harvested marijuana buds is a sight that few people ever get the chance to see. Pot lovers all over the world might dream about such a sight, but it takes a real entrepreneur to make those dreams come true.

After the buds have been dried, they are ready to be "manicured," which means the small leaves around the buds are trimmed away with scissors and shaped into attractive and similar items. Drying and trimming properly, along with picking the right seed stock, will give us the best chance to get the top price for our crop. The first time I witnessed two hundred pounds of buds shrink down to one hundred pounds, I wanted to cry, but I didn't understand farming and the process that agricultural products went through on their way to the marketplace. Understanding this principle of weight loss is essential for the farmer when he is planning his profit, whether his crop is grown in the closet or in the field.

I was wondering how Don and I were going to trim a hundred pounds by ourselves, but he had an answer for that problem too. He hired his maid and two of her girlfriends at $10 an hour to trim buds; apparently this had been a ritual for the past five years. It wasn't an uncommon thing for locals to do during harvest time on the Mendocino coast.

Since Don's new bedroom didn't have any furniture in it, we spread plastic sheets on the floor and placed newspaper on top of that. The girls sat on the floor in a circle, with a mound of buds in front of them, and they placed the trimmed product in paper bags. Don and I would weigh the buds, put them into one-pound ziplock bags, and place them in the refrigerator to keep fresh. We filled the wheelbarrow with buds ten times to bring all the harvest into the room. This process took us two nights and three days. Of course the girls passed the pipe and listened to music while enjoying the spirit of being part of the whole independent experience. Smoking good pot and making tax-free money was a dream come true for them and their families. I should correct myself by saying that these weren't girls; they were women who were probably in their late thirties or early forties. They had husbands working in the community as plumbers, electricians, and real-estate agents. They were homemakers with children, who needed to keep up with the rising cost of school supplies, clothes, and food that the government seemed to have forgotten about while spending on their war on drugs.

The subculture of marijuana growers is a very tight community network of dedicated people who depend upon honor and commitment with each other and with their business transactions. The cannabis industry is self-regulated; people who prove to be untrustworthy or dishonest will find it impossible to do business in the community—which is more than we can say for our leaders in Washington.

Before I tell you what it's like to sell a hundred pounds of marijuana, I think you should know a little more about the people in the industry. There are millions of American citizens who are making a comfortable living growing buds to supplement their income. They pay the mortgages on their homes, buy cars, pay their taxes, open small businesses, pay tithes to their churches, and donate to community charities. This money makes a significant impact on the economy, and the bigger the cannabis industry is, the more impact it has on the health of this nation. This is the dirty little secret our politicians don't want you to know about—but more than that, they really don't want you to know how easy it is to stand on your own two feet and rule yourself.

Those entrepreneurs who have the courage and determination not to let a corrupt government stand in the way of their pursuit of happiness have created a multibillion-dollar industry that is keeping our country from imploding. Motivation, opportunity, and courage blaze the road to happiness, not wealth, power, and position. The cannabis industry doesn't have a political agenda; it doesn't need one world order or social justice. All it's doing is making things right again and healing this nation from the outside in, right out in the open, in full view of anyone who has the eyes to look for it. But unless you have the courage and determination to find the truth for yourself, you'll never be able to take the blinders off. Don't take my word for it. Do your own studies.

Meanwhile, back at Don's barn up in the country, a quarter-million-dollar deal was about to take place. A hundred pounds of dried buds x $2,500 bulk price = $250,000 tax-free money.

$250,000 divided into 60 percent and 40 percent = $150,000 for Don and $100,000 for the neophyte.

Since I was the student and none of the buyers knew who I was, my job was to stay out of sight and back Don up in case something went wrong. As the Boy Scouts say, it's always best to be prepared; one never knows when something will go wrong. Doing the Tiburon shuffle for many years, I'd heard rumors about deals going south, but then again, I'd never been involved with such a large amount of money. Don told me that he had worked with these men several times before and never had any problems. Then he handed me a 9 mm pistol and said that it was always better to be safe than sorry. He opened the closet door and nudged me inside. My job was to watch the transaction and come to the rescue if something went wrong. Should I, would I, could I, shoot someone if the deal went sour? Was I ready, willing, and able to kill another human being over something I had worked so hard to achieve?

Would George Washington shoot someone for trying to rob his crop? Would Patrick Henry kill for free enterprise? How much money would it take for you to shoot another human being? If someone paid you a million dollars in counterfeit money for your hard-earned business, would you put a hole in his head? These are the questions I was asking myself as I stood in that closet waiting for the buyers to arrive. And these are the questions you need to ask yourself if you decide to go into business in the cannabis industry, because there are bad people out there on both sides of the table. I guess, in the end, if push came to shove, I would probably put a bullet hole so deep in someone they would need a telescope to see where it landed. And just like tinnitus, I would learn how to live with it. But fortunately for me, I didn't have to make that choice, and all those bad thoughts I was thinking crawled back into their hole and went back to sleep. But make no mistake about it, I came to these terms a long time ago. If you come into my life with the intention of bringing harm to me or my family, you will reap the benefits of your own misfortune.

Two vehicles came down the driveway, a black Subaru Outback with two men inside and a white Chevy van with two women. The van had a sign on the side that said Mill Valley School District Book Depository. Don stood in the doorway and shook hands as all four guest entered the barn. The two men followed him to the refrigerators and watched as he unlocked the doors and then stood to the side as the men inspected the one-pound bags. After a few minutes, they took one bag from each refrigerator and placed the bags on the table so they could get a better look under the light. They took a handful of buds from each bag and closely inspected them with a magnifying glass, checking for smell, color, and crystal density. The two buyers were smiling and rolling their eyes with excitement. I heard them say "wow" and "beautiful" several times as they licked their sticky fingers. Don asked if they would like to sample the product, and one of the men filled a small pipe and handed it to one of the women, who took a couple of tokes. After a few minutes, she grinned with satisfaction and admitted that she had taken one hit too many, and they all started to laugh. One of the men went out to the car, brought back a brown leather suitcase, and placed it on the table. The other man took a key and opened it for Don to inspect. I couldn't see from where I was standing, but I later learned there were fifty bundles of five thousand dollars each. Don picked up a stack, took the rubber bands off, and fanned the bills out like a deck of cards. The money was all there, and not one word was ever spoken about the price. They trusted Don so well that all they wanted to know was how many pounds he had produced.

Don took the money out of the suitcase, put it in a canvas bag, and then placed it under the table. The three men shook hands again, and the two women began to pack the pounds into white boxes marked English Department and then seal them with packing tape. When one of the refrigerators was empty, Don took the money and locked it inside. He asked the group whether they wanted to stay for lunch, but they declined, saying that they needed to get back to Marin county before the last class. After they had loaded the boxes into the van, they got back in their vehicles and drove away. The whole transaction had taken less than twenty minutes.

I walked out of the closet when Don came back into the barn, and we hugged each other and then spontaneously started to dance around the barn in some sort of ancient caveman ritual. We were realizing that the American dream, in all of its splendid glory, was still alive and well for those who were brave enough to pursuit it for themselves. When things calmed down, Don unlocked the refrigerator and placed fifty bundles of pure hard-earned cash on the table in front of us. Then he counted out twenty stacks and moved them over to the edge of the table in front of me. One hundred thousand dollars of tax-free money sitting on a table inside a barn isn't something the average citizen gets to see in a lifetime. My first thought was, *If I could grow a hundred pounds I could grow four hundred pounds—and that's all I need to make my first million dollars.* I reached around my back, and pulled out the 9 mm pistol. I took out the clip and then ejected the round in the chamber. I placed the gun on the table and said that I wished I had had that gun when those two banjo players were firing rounds over our heads in the garden. Our laughter was a mixture of relief and joy. We knew that our project in the woods was over but the bonds of our friendship would last forever. I learned right then that the bonds of trust and courage are earned, not given, and that the future of this country is determined by individuals, not groups of politicians.

Those pounds that we sold for $2,500 apiece would bring $5,000 to $8,000 each out on the streets. That's enough profit to go around for everyone, and that's why, after declaring war on drugs and causing so much damage to the American people, big business is now lobbying the government to help them legalize marijuana so they, too, can get their sticky fingers on some of the profits. Fortunately for the cannabis industry, the government can only control a small part of the medical marijuana market by taxing the dispensaries and regulating a small group of licensed growers. Everyone who knows anything about marijuana will tell you that there's no difference between casual use and medical marijuana. With the collusion between big business and big government, the Madison Avenue marketers have created a new propaganda-advertising and public-relations scheme called Medical Marijuana. They have sold the idea to the American people as a legitimate industry, but the truth is that the medical buds come from the same cannabis plants that everyone else is smoking.

The American people can grow their own "medical marijuana" without help from their government. Do you know anything at all about what happens when a doctor writes a prescription for marijuana? The prescription is basically a license for the patient to purchase marijuana from a state-run dispensary; as well, the patient has the legal right to grow ten mature female pot plants and twenty immature plants in the privacy of his or her own home or in a caregiver's home. He or she can use whichever marijuana seeds they choose to buy. Medical patients have been self-medicating without their doctor's permission for as long as the Marijuana Prohibition Act has been punishing the citizens of this country.

It's the elderly who are really the victims of this medical marijuana scheme, because if they live in a state that doesn't have "medical marijuana" laws, the doctors are pushing a pharmaceutical synthetic drug that mimics the benefits of the natural marijuana plant but doesn't deliver the same results—and the patients aren't being told that they have a choice. Consumers can grow their own marijuana more economically than the government can, but the elderly are often under the restrictions of hospitals and retirement homes, where doctors and nurses feel no obligation to explain marijuana benefits to their patients. The point is, the government and big business have been in bed with each other for over a hundred years, trying very successfully to control every aspect of our daily lives. They are destroying the foundation of this republic. That's a big secret as to why the cannabis industry is one of the most successful industries in American history: it's because the people of this nation have found a livelihood that allows them to stand on their own two feet and rule themselves. Don't take my word for it. Do your own research, and stop listening to what the government is saying—because they're not telling you the truth.

It was Sunday afternoon, and a quarter of a million dollars was stacked neatly on the table in front of Don and me, one hundred and fifty thousand dollars on one side, and a hundred thousand on the other. I told Don that I didn't like the idea of driving around with a hundred thousand dollars in my car, and I was wondering how I could keep it safe until I could decide how to spend it without alarming the authorities. Don suggested that I take ten thousand out and keep the rest in the underground safe that he had buried on his property. He had showed me his "safe" before, and I knew exactly where it was located. (The safe was a plastic pickle barrel, about the size of a thirty-three-gallon trash can, except it had a screw-down lid that kept moisture from getting in or out of the barrel.) We placed all of the money except for my ten thousand dollars in ziplock bags and placed it in the safe. We screwed the lid down tight and covered the top of the barrel with about six inches of dirt and sand. We placed an old pine stump over the safe and scattered rocks around the edges. It was one of the best-kept secrets of hidden money that I had ever seen. We shook hands, and I put the $10,000 in my backpack and drove home. I was thinking to myself what a long, hard trip it had been to accomplish my first outdoor grow.

I wish I could say that was the end of the story, but it wasn't. Two days later, I went back to Don's house to have some coffee and brag about our successful harvest and discovered that my worst nightmare had come true. The cars were gone, the house was empty, and the safe was nothing but an empty hole in the ground. The housekeeper said that Don had moved his family to Washington state. They must have been planning this for a long time, because they made a clean getaway. It was a sad and difficult lesson for me to learn but a perfect example of how trusting someone isn't enough—especially when it comes to growing a secret garden in the wilderness. This was a person whom I had known for over thirty years; we traveled and worked together and yet trusting him as a partner still hadn't been enough. For days I walked around thinking of all the different ways I was going to kill Don. Even today the emotional residue of his deception continues to punch me in the spiritual solar plexus. I'm telling you this story because you need to understand that trust and courage aren't enough when it comes to making a million dollars in the cannabis industry. One of the biggest secrets no one is telling about the drug war is that it's not the action of the cannabis plant but the behavior of individual human beings that is so terrible.

The Grow

By Chuck Allen Jr

It's a two-mile hike up a sandy creek bed;
Take the fork to the left, then go straight ahead.
Look for a willow on the side of a hill;
Go under the branches, and follow it still.

Try not to let your footprints be seen;
It's hard to be found if the trail is clean.
Don't smoke or eat along the way;
One mistake could ruin your day.

Follow the creek till you find a pool,
Crystal clear and wonderfully full;
Check the filter to clear the line;
A dead salamander could cost you time.

Follow the pipeline back to the west;
On the side of the hill the garden grows best.
Check the fence to see if it's broken;
The timer is dead, and I'm not joking.

A little fertilizer next to the emitter;
A sleepy snake is a nasty critter.
Check the holes for water breaks
And any other costly mistakes.

Take a break and have some lunch;
Then check the buds on a hunch.
The red furry fibers are turning to brown;
No finer garden could ever be found.

Harvest the crop in a couple of hours;
Remember to pick only the flowers.
A bag on my shoulder in both of my hands;
Back to the truck as fast as I can.

Dry the buds in brown paper bags;
The best secret garden that I've ever had.
I'll go back to the grow year after year,
As long as my intentions stay crystal clear.

CHAPTER 5

The Secret of Muzzo's Pizza Shop

When the boss is gone, and no one is looking,
I sprinkle marijuana on the pizza I'm cooking

Mr. Muzzo was a professor of mathematics at a leading California University. He wasn't a liberal person at all; in fact, he was a conservative man who believed in traditional values and principles. Some of his students found him soft spoken and sometimes difficult to hear, but he was a brilliant teacher, with a wonderful sense of humor.

Muzzo's hobby was going to yard sales, garage sales, and estate sales in his spare time, looking for old mechanical equipment, toys, and electrical devices that were long past their usefulness. His passion was tinkering with those items and finding ways to rebuild, reconstruct, or simply fix them to his satisfaction.

One day he came across something that he couldn't figure out. It had cranks, pulleys, rollers, and belts that didn't make any sense to him. There didn't seem to be any rhyme or reason to its function. For a year he kept picking it up and then putting it aside again in confusion. He replaced all the moving parts and polished and oiled the machine until it looked new, but still he had to meditate over it with no answers. Then, one day, he plugged the contraception in, and as he watched the moving parts, he had an epiphany. The crazy device was nothing but a pizza machine, designed to flatten out pizza dough without tossing it around in the air and catching it with the knuckles. All the cook had to do was roll the dough into the desired size ball, sprinkle it with some cornstarch, drop it between the moving rollers, and bingo-bango, it came out the other side all flattened and ready to be trimmed to the desired shape.

Muzzo got so excited with his newfound invention that he started to make his own pizza and take it to class with him for lunch. Over time he developed his own sourdough mix, his own tomato sauce, and his own special blend of three-cheese toppings (1/3 mozzarella, 1/3 Romano, and 1/3 provolone).

Before long, Muzzo's students were begging him to share bites and slices with his class. They didn't care that it was cold; they loved it anyway. Muzzo's pizza became the rave of the campus, and one student was making a profit selling Muzzo T-shirts. One day Muzzo was approached by a group of businessmen wanting him to open a pizza shop inside the student-union building on campus. Ordinarily, people would approach banks for financing new businesses, but these businessmen were so impressed with his popularity that they saw big dollar signs with possible franchise opportunities in the near future. They were willing to handle all the paperwork and deal with the college bureaucracy, if he would be willing to start a small pizza business under his name, with full rights for all his ideas. All he would have to do was supervise the start-up, do the training, and then let the students run the business. He would be the owner-boss and call all the shots. He would still maintain his class schedule and receive a 40 percent take of the profits, with the remaining proceeds going to the student-union organization. The business would be strictly a take-out, with no tables or chairs or dish machine to maintain. The major health-code requirements would be simple: a handicap-accessible restroom, a three-basin sink with hot water, a commercial walk-in refrigerator, and separate storage rooms for cooking and cleaning supplies. The biggest expense would be a commercial gas pizza oven, which would cost $20,000.

It was a deal too good for a sixty-two-year-old man to pass up. After all, how difficult could it be to run a small pizza shop? Legal steps were taken for ownership of the Muzzo business name, the company logo, and all the rights and privileges concerning patents for the menu, recipes, and the pizza-dough machine. The final agreement stated that Muzzo's Pizza Shop, located in the student union building, was to be officially recognized as an organization independent of the educational facility. A percentage of the proceeds was to be given to the student union organization to help support student activities both on the local and national levels. Other proceeds were to come from the sale of only one item from the menu, exclusively sold as a "student special." This item must be sold only to students with a student ID. All other items on the menu were to be sold to the facility, staff, and the general public without restrictions. The representatives of the student union were to use the funds to support the goals and services of the student union organization.

Muzzo didn't support all the activities of the student union, but he agreed to sign the contract because he believed that Muzzo's Pizza Shop would make a lot of people happy and him a rich man in the process.

Contractors were hired and a suitable location on the ground floor of the student union building was agreed upon. Equipment was installed, and vendors were contacted. Menus were printed and supplies ordered. Muzzo designed the logo for the pizza shop, which was a simple round white sign with a sketch of a chef's hat with two eyes and a mustache sticking out like cat whiskers. Underneath the sketch were green block letters that said, Muzzo's Pizza Shop. Friendly Eating.

The president of the student union was contacted, and arrangements were made for interviews to hire and train students before the grand opening.

The pizza shop would be open seven days a week from 10 a.m. until 6 p.m., with one hour for cleaning after closing. This worked out perfectly for everyone, because not all students went home on the weekends, and pizza was available every day. Muzzo was the manager and did all the hiring and firing. The supervisor did the training, ordering, and schedules. The crew leader made sure all the other employees came to work on time and watched portion control. Everyone except Muzzo did the cooking and worked a rotating schedule.

Unfortunately for Muzzo, he was unable to do the interviewing himself because of exam week and scheduling conflicts, so the president of the student union did the hiring for him. And when Muzzo arrived at the pizza shop to meet his new supervisor, he was shocked to see the most radical student on campus sitting behind the office desk. Pedro O'Malley was a thirty-seven-year-old left-wing extremist who considered himself a social democrat, but he was really a progressive communist at heart. His real name was Peter, but he was so dedicated to helping the illegal aliens from Mexico regain the land that had been stolen from them by the American Republican party that he changed it to Pedro to honor the cause. Everyone on campus knew him from one demonstration or another. He was a professional student with a major in liberal arts, who spent most of his time smoking pot, drinking tequila, and giving yoga classes to his constituents. His head was bald except for a green spiky Mohawk that stood eight inches tall; it was his statement flag for the shock generation. Pedro was a straight-A student who knew the tricks of taking a test; unfortunately, none of the tests were in American history or common sense. By the time Muzzo walked into Pedro's office, a revolutionary plan had already been hatched in which Pedro was the new Che. Muzzo decided right there on the spot that after the training, he would let Pedro run the whole damn show; he didn't want anything to do with it. Pedro took over the shop and Muzzo took all the credit, which was the way it should be, but it really wasn't.

Pedro's plan was right out of the communist handbook: use fear and anger to collapse the system from within. All the money taken in from the sales of the "Student Specials" would go directly into the student-fund account, which he now controlled. His plan was to skim money from the account and make a million dollars that he could use to control the thirty-five thousand students roaming his campus. His idea included a scheme that he had been dreaming about for years, something so wild and controversial that people would remember his name forever. Everyone knows that college students smoke a lot of pot, especially at university. His idea was to sprinkle marijuana instead of oregano on the "Student Special" pizzas, without telling anyone, and only those students who bought the "special" would understand how special it really was. He would use his Mexican connections to supply the marijuana and substitute the pot for the oregano in the privacy of his own apartment. Once the word got around campus about how special the pizza really was, sales would skyrocket, and his dream would come true. But the beautiful part about the plan was the ending. He knew that eventually his scheme would be discovered, and the students would be angry and fearful that Muzzo's Pizza Shop would be closed, and then they would take their bitterness and resentment to the streets and blame the conservative right-wing establishment for taking away their right to eat marijuana if they wanted to. They would claim freedom of choice to eat marijuana if they choose to and the right to put into their bodies whichever herbs they desired, for medicinal purposes or not. Hopefully it would go all the way to the Supreme Court, where the liberal judges would make a landmark decision in their favor, and his marijuana-pizza idea would make his controversial story a *New York Times* best seller.

Most people don't understand the difference between eating marijuana and smoking it. It's like the difference between wine and whiskey; one gets you drunk faster than the other. When marijuana is smoked, it goes through the respiratory system; if it's eaten, it goes through the circulatory system. One way it goes instantly into the bloodstream through the lungs; the other it has to be digested through the stomach and then go into the bloodstream. But the most important difference is the intensity and duration of the high. Marijuana that's smoked generally lasts three or four hours, but if it's eaten, the effect is intensified and can last eight to ten hours, depending on how much was consumed.

Anyway, campus administrators, teachers, and professors wouldn't understand at first what the civilian authorities were talking about, because they couldn't buy the special pizzas, not having student ID cards. This would give Pedro a potential thirty-five-thousand-student fan club and make them willing victims of his wonderfully delicious marijuana pizza scheme, which they all enjoyed and no one wanted to give up. It would be their pizza fight, and other student union organizations across the nation would support their cause. Global student unions would join the fight in the streets and be more than willing to stomp on the US Constitution in front of the mass-media propaganda machine.

Pedro picked May 5, Cinco de Mayo, for the grand opening of Muzzo's Pizza Shop, and it was the perfect occasion for the misunderstanding of the Mexican Independence Day. There would be thousands of students eating pizza and getting stoned; he couldn't think of a better way to introduce Muzzo's pizza to the world. All the countless hours he'd spent cleaning pot would soon pay him a big reward.

Pedro was a true revolutionary. He understood the progressive thought process and knew that when the teachers' union voted for tenure in academia, it opened the door for radical revolutionaries to teach openly in the classroom that socialism and communism was a better form of government than the Constitution and the republic. He also understood that when politicians voted to remove term limits for themselves, they welcomed subversion and treason into the kitchen of public opinion and poisoned the stew.

Muzzo kept himself busy in the classroom and only came to the pizza shop on short visits to greet the customers or to clean the pizza machine. With his popularity on the rise and his pizzas the topic of conversation all over campus, he realized that he'd better build one or two more pizza machines, in case the one they had broke down for more than a day.

Pedro bought cases of oregano and kept them openly on the shelf in the storage room, but the marijuana was kept in a large metal shaker, which was filled only by him each morning. The special pizzas were so popular that a second worktable had to be built just for the preparation of those pizzas. Pedro made sure the marijuana was removed from the building at the end of each day. He worked seven days a week to make sure his scheme ran smoothly, but he only reported forty hours, to keep his paycheck within reason. None of the other employees suspected what was going on until they started to eat the special pizza on their lunch break—and then the sound system was turned up and the work environment became much more enjoyable.

At the end of the first month, Muzzo's Pizza grossed over $50,000, averaging about $12,250 a week. After taxes, that left $33,500 to pay the bank, payroll, food cost, and maintenance costs. That left $21,500 to be split 60/40 between the student union and Mr. Muzzo ($12,900 for the union, $8,600 for Muzzo). After taxes, Muzzo could expect to deposit $5,762, plus his teaching salary, every month. Not bad for a man approaching his retirement years.

Pedro was receiving his weekly paycheck of $486 plus a dollar for each special pizza that he sold. Here's how his scam worked. He programmed the cash register for a dollar more on one key and the regular menu price on another key for the same special, and at the end of the day he would count the number of specials sold and pocket the difference. If someone complained, he would void the transaction and push in the correct price. But the truth is that 99.99 percent of the time the students were too busy, too distracted, or too stoned to care about the price. With the pizza shop being open seven days a week and averaging over a hundred special sales a day, Pedro was making about $1,186 a week, $4,744 a month, or $56,928 a year. In ten years he would make $500,000, and in twenty years he could retire with a cool million dollars. All it would take was to sprinkle a few grams of marijuana on pizza.

But Pedro had much bigger plans than that. He didn't want to wait twenty years to make his first million; he wanted to make it much sooner than that. If he could convince Muzzo to open another pizza shop in the student union buildings at UCLA, Stanford, and San Francisco State, his dream of making a million dollars from selling marijuana pizza would happen in less than two years. If Muzzo paid him a salary and made him district manager, he could program the registers, do the deposits, quadruple his income, and retire a multimillionaire in a very short period of time. And the best part of his plan was that he knew that if he ever got caught by the pigs, the students would rally all the other student union organizations and take to the streets, spreading fear and intimidation, to show their support. He would become a revolutionary hero, and write a book, and become even richer!

After a year doing business, Muzzo's Pizza Shop had a financial track record that was the envy of any fast food restaurant on record in the state. The quality of the food and the popularity of the name showed all the signs of becoming a dynamic organization.

Unfortunately for Pedro, the bankers had a different idea for Muzzo's Pizza Shop, and his big scheme to embezzle money from the system by using marijuana pizzas came crashing down around his head. The businessmen believed that Muzzo's Pizza Shop was ready to franchise, and they wanted to make it strictly carry-out, with a drive-up window, and perhaps add fresh sandwiches, French fries, soups, chili, homemade cornbread, and chocolate cake to the menu. When the group of bankers approached Muzzo and offered him $1.3 million for the rights to his business, he saw the opportunity to retire a wealthy man and took it. He really wasn't a businessman and certainly not a restaurant manager. He didn't mind teaching, but he didn't feel comfortable dealing with customers and employees. So, after two years, Muzzo sold his business name, logo, recipes, inventory, and two pizza machines. They would pay him a handsome fee to build more pizza machines as they opened new franchises. The investors wanted the original pizza shop to stay on campus in the student union building and offered them a five-year lease. They felt that the location brought good advertising and public relations to the franchise.

Pedro the revolutionary wasn't a happy camper. He was still making good money, but he would be working the system for another twenty years before he reached his goal of making a million dollars selling marijuana pizza. So he came up with a new idea: buy a student special pizza and receive a T-shirt with bold green letters that said Muzzo's Premo Pizza across the front, for only ten dollars. He could buy a package of three white T-shirts at Walmart for three dollars, then stencil and paint would cost another two bucks, and his profit would be five dollars a shirt. If he sold ten T-shirts a day, that would be $50 dollars a day, $350 a week, or $18,200 a year. In ten years he would make $182,000.

At first the T-shirt idea worked very well. The students loved the play on words, Premo Pizza, Premo Pot, but after a few weeks sales dropped from ten or twenty a day to one or two a day, and Pedro's marketing idea sailed off the edge of the horizon. Students were not eating the student special as much anymore, because they were tired of being stoned all the time. Once in a while they just wanted a good pizza at a reasonable price, without the mysterious ingredient. A lot of students were on a budget, and every dollar that they spent on fast food made a difference. Muzzo's pizza was still a great pizza but not the student special.

Pedro's income dropped sharply, and the student union's activity director began to receive complaints about the so-called students' special that wasn't so special. Pedro heard through his revolutionary grapevine that an internal investigation was about to happen any day, so he cleaned out all the marijuana in the pizza shop and reprogrammed the cash register to reflect the menu price. When security did their inspection of the business, they found nothing wrong. It was a close call for Pedro, but he had still made almost $150,000 tax-free in two years.

Meanwhile, back at the bank, a patent attorney informed the investors that Mr. Muzzo's pizza machine didn't belong to him; he hadn't invented it and didn't hold a patent on the machine. What was interesting in the attorney's report was that a Mr. G. W. Schlinhten had invented the machine in 1915, two years before he invented a hemp-harvesting machine that would have revolutionized the hemp industry the same way the cotton gin revolutionized the cotton industry. Unfortunately, Mr. Schlinhten mysteriously disappeared, along with his hemp harvester and the pizza machine (he called it a dough machine). According to the patent office, there were gaps in the records and paperwork, for newer and improved machines didn't appear until many years after Mr. Schlinhten disappeared. The attorney strongly recommended not spending money trying to seek the patent on such an old and outdated machine but to just purchase pizza machines that were more suitable for the modern fast-food industry.

Back at the students' union building, Pedro was rapidly running out of places to hide. His apartment had been searched and two pounds of pot found hidden in his closet. Evidence was mounting that customers had been overcharged on his shift, and DEA agents were looking to question him about possible connections with the drug cartels in Mexico. Things were starting to fall apart fast, but Pedro had one last plan for his redemption. He withdrew all his savings, collected all his cash, and bought a used Chevy van to carry his meager belongings. Then he shaved his green Mohawk, put on a blond wig, took his key to the shop, and stole the pizza machine. He loaded everything into the van, drove across the Bay Bridge, through San Francisco, across the Golden Gate Bridge, and didn't stop until he reached the small town of Jenner on the northern California coast, where he ran out of gas. He had almost a quarter of a million dollars hidden in the van and nowhere else to go.

The next morning, Pedro met a dingy waitress named Destiny, whose mother owned the restaurant, father owned the gas station, and aunt and uncle owned the antique store across the street. They fell in love at a dirty table overlooking the Pacific Ocean. He changed his name back to Peter, she found her destiny with him, and together they bought a portable vending trailer, complete with electric oven, refrigerator, kitchen sink, and porta potty. They hooked the trailer up to the Chevy van and started selling pizzas up and down Highway 1 between Jenner and Fort Bragg. They used Muzzo's recipes for their sourdough mix, tomato sauce, and three-cheese toppings. And, of course, they had the pizza machine. They named their new business Pete's Pizza Pie—Your Destiny to Adventure. They cooked fresh pizza pies for tourist and locals who were looking for that chance to taste a piece of the American pie.

But that's not the end of the story. One day they were plugged into the electrical outlet at the Safeway parking lot in Fort Bragg, cooking pizzas, when Pete had this revolutionary idea. Although there were many pot growers in the area, there wasn't a store in town selling equipment and supplies for their needs. They had to drive two hours to buy indoor growing supplies; there seemed to be a market for the idea. There just happened to be a vacant building next door to the Safeway supermarket, and they were able to negotiate with the owner for a very reasonable lease. The idea was to not only sell equipment and supplies but to also offer information that would help people organize their thoughts about the cannabis industry. They applied for and received a state license to open a dispensary for medical marijuana. They also opened a bakery specializing in marijuana recipes and a bookstore that sold tapes and videos related to the industry. They named their new business Gro Smart, and it quickly became a local phenomenon. Within two years, they started selling franchises all over California and became one of this country's richest entrepreneurs.

Unfortunately for Pedro and his dingy girlfriend, the economy took a nosedive, his franchise business went into bankruptcy, and Pedro ended up selling hot dogs on the side of the road in southern Oregon. But the cannabis industry has a way of taking care of one of its own, and Pedro continued to sell buds to tourist visiting the local ski resort.

Muzzo's Pizza Shop

By Chuck Allen Jr.

Years ago I moved to a small town;
The view of the city was the best around.
I worked for a professor from UC Berkeley,
A mathematician who was kind of quirky.

He invented a machine that flattened out dough,
All sizes of pizza, row after row.
He opened a restaurant but called it a shop,
Making his pizzas that everyone bought.

With tables out front and the kitchen in back,
You could also take home your food in a sack.
The manager was cursed with a very red face;
He was allergic to working with tomato paste.

Sometimes the customer had a bad attitude,
Being mean and loud and often rude.
When the boss was gone, and no one was looking,
I sprinkled marijuana on the pizza when cooking.

A red tablecloth, with some candles and wine,
Set the stage for amusement I had on my mind.
Those macho jerks who treated their date
With angry control that was verging on hate

Would suddenly find their contentious bone,
Changing the venue and smoothing their tone.
The pot did more than just add to the flavor;
It gave to the couple a wonderful favor.

I cooked in the kitchen with purpose and flair,
Sprinkling pot on their pizza without any care.
I delivered the food with style and grace,
Then watched the change come over their face.

For a moment in time there would be a chance
For their dinner to end in a hopeful romance.
The couple did leave while holding their hands,
Never once suspecting my marijuana plans.

Muzzo's Pizza Shop said the green-and-white sign
Hanging high above the sidewalk suspended in time.
A thin-crusted pizza, from a sourdough crock,
Cooked to perfection with some homegrown pot.

CHAPTER 6

The Secret Garden of a Postal Worker

Down in the basement, in back of the room,
Is a secret garden that I will harvest soon.

Leavenworth is a small town in northeastern Kansas, which is historically known as the first city of Kansas. When most people think of Kansas, they visualize rolling plains and wheat fields as far as the eye can see, but Leavenworth isn't like that at all. Her thirty thousand residents move back and forth between work and home under the canopy of majestic pin oaks and silver maple trees that line the hilly streets. The city has a rich background in military history, and her future is a constant battle between liberal and conservative thought. Today the progressives are winning the war, right under the nose of some of the best generals in the army. Just like those pioneers who kept pushing their agendas across that muddy river and heading toward that setting sun in the West, a steady stream of progressive thought has infected the military without firing a shot. Wearing their camouflage uniforms in the civilian world is the antithesis of what the purpose of camouflage is all about. Instead of blending in with traditional military uniforms, they stand out in contrast of who they are—progressive idiots pretending that the enemy can't see who they are.

But not all of the residents of Leavenworth have been brainwashed. I'm thinking of a dedicated working man named Thomas Joe-bob Floyd, who carved himself out a niche inside the US Postal Service. Unlike most of his neighbors, Thomas had traveled beyond the Kansas borders and had a different perspective of the world around him. He was a pot smoker and had been one ever since he joined the army in 1966. He was one of those people who actually knew what he was talking about when it came to the topic of marijuana, in spite of what the military and the government were trying to make him believe. Thomas listened to the teachers, and the pundits, and the doctors, and the lawyers—and their opinions didn't match up with his experience of the real world. Marijuana wasn't the monster that they wanted him to believe. Somehow, someway, someone was using the mass media to spread propaganda and lies about a plant that was more beneficial than it was harmful. How this could happen in the United States was of great concern to Thomas, but he just kept minding his own business and doing what he thought was right, including smoking his pot.

After the army, he took a civil-service class and went to work for the post office, making over $50,000 a year delivering the mail in a town where the average income was less than $20,000. He knew almost everyone by their first name—and their kids' names and their pets' names. Thomas was forty-seven and had been working for the government for twenty years, which was longer than most people had been married. If you want to know how to make a million dollars in the cannabis industry, Thomas had a story that would make a good example.

Early in his career, he bought a house on a very quiet street in the upscale part of town. It was a two-story brick colonial at the end of a cul-de-sac, with two giant pin oaks on the front lawn. Garden ivy climbed the brick walls on both sides of the screened-in front porch. The oversized lot had a fenced backyard with a mix of thirty-year-old trees providing shade for his patio. His neighbors were elderly and retired, and they all knew him as the friendly mailman from the First Methodist Church. But little did they know that Thomas had a secret garden in the basement of his house that was making more money than most of the doctors and lawyers in town. His courage and desire to be an entrepreneur helped him develop skills that impacted the lives of hundreds of Kansas citizens on a daily basis. Let's take a moment to do some math, so you'll understand what I'm talking about. Thomas was growing one pound a month and selling sixteen ounces at $300 each.

16 ounces x $300 = $4,800 a month

$4,800 a month x 12 months = $57,600 a year

See how fast that adds up? Add $57,600 to his post-office salary of $50,000, and that equals

$107,600 a year, give or take a few thousand for taxes, etc.

$107,600 x 10 years = $1,076,000

$1,076,000 x 20 = $2,152,000

Are you impressed yet? He became a multimillionaire in twenty years just from growing one pound of dried marijuana buds in the basement of his own home. Now, I'm not saying that growing pot is for everyone, because obviously it's not, but Thomas had the courage, the determination, the principles, and the values necessary to get the job done.

Those are the qualities that every entrepreneur must have to be successful, and he doesn't need permission from the Supreme Court, because his products are contributing significantly to the economy in a positive and meaningful way, regardless of some people's strongly held opinions to the contrary. Having said that, let's get back to Thomas Joe-bob Floyd's story.

Not only was he a millionaire, unknown to the town, but he also volunteered his time and money to community projects and church programs. He played the piano for senior citizens in long-term care facilities, taught bible school at his church, volunteered for Habitat for Humanity programs, and coached softball for the local youth groups. At the end of the day, after dinner, after the garden was tended, after he put a movie in the VCR, after he poured himself a glass of wine and took the phone off the hook, he would take a few puffs from his homegrown herb and reflect on the day's activities.

As radio host Paul Harvey used to say, "Now for the rest of the story." Thomas was an accomplished cook, some might say an extraordinary chef of specialty delights. He spent years in the kitchen perfecting his marijuana recipes for candies and desserts. He could have made an additional fortune selling those desserts, but instead he decided to give them away to nurses working in the long-term care facilities and private nursing homes in the community. His piano-playing brought about opportunities to meet several concerned nurses who had patients inquiring about the medical benefits of marijuana but didn't know where to find it. Through discreet conversations with the nurses, he told them that he knew someone who might be able to help, because this person made marijuana candy, cookies, and brownies. This was better for the patients, because there would be no smoke to alarm someone who might disagree with their choice of medical solution. After further discussions, the nurses decided that they needed to check with the individual patients' medical charts to see if there were any diabetics, smoke allergies, or patients with any other medical condition that could keep them from eating cannabis food.

Thomas went home and thought seriously about how he could positively impact the lives of people who were suffering from physical and emotional pain, as well as those who had sleep disorders or who found it difficult to eat after cancer treatment. He decided that if he made only marijuana candy, like caramel wraps, peppermint drops, lemon drops, and chocolate drops, he could control the potency. He decided that he wouldn't charge a dime. It would be his way of giving back to the community without anyone knowing.

The next time Thomasd went to the piano sing-along, he told the head nurse that he had brought a one-pound bag of medical chocolate caramels with him and informed her that the candy would be free from now on; it was the cook's way of giving back to the community. He told her that the candy would take between forty-five minutes and an hour to take effect and that it was medium in strength. If she had patients that needed to increase the strength, she was to let him know how much and how many, and he would take care of it. When Thomas returned for his piano sing-along the next week, the head nurse took him aside and thanked him profusely for the service he was providing. She had noticed significant increases in appetite, less joint and muscle pain, less stress and anxiety and, above all, an increase in the quality of sleep her patients were receiving.

As Paul Harvey's son used to say, "Now for the rest of the story." After a year of dating, Thomas and the head nurse got married. They seemed to share so much in common: their commitment to helping others, their desire to serve the community, their enjoyment of old movies, a crackling fireplace, a good glass of wine, and the puff from a spicy bud. But it's hard to keep a garden in the basement a secret from your wife. In the beginning she was cool with it; she thought it was exciting and adventuresome, but after a while she flipped. I guess *flipped* doesn't describe it well enough; what she really did was step off the train they both were riding and bought a ticket for a jet trip to another universe. With all the sex and the pot and the other stuff that was going on, Thomas had forgotten that his wife's father was a county judge at the local courthouse. He kept trying to get her to relax and enjoy the situation, but the truth about her bipolar condition kept coming around and biting him in the ass. He was in deep voodoo and couldn't see any way out, except the complete abandonment of everything he had worked so hard to achieve in life. So, without notice, he withdrew half of his savings from the bank, collected his stash of money hidden in the backyard, and moved to the Florida Keys. He left her the house and the divorce to deal with and never looked back. He opened a barbecue rib shack on the beach and lived on a houseboat in a popular marina.

I met Thomas while on a fishing trip in the Florida Keys one summer. My fishing buddies and I stopped in his barbecue joint, and he told us this story over pulled pork sandwiches and a cold beer. As sad as his story was, Floyd had a great sense of humor, and he concluded our visit with this thought: He said that the moral of his story was that none of this had anything to do with marijuana being the monster in our society and everything to do with the corruption of the human condition. Good or bad, the citizens of this country have the ability to rule themselves.

The Closet

By Chuck Allen Jr.

Down in the basement, in back of the room,
Is a secret garden I will harvest soon.
Five-gallon buckets with holes in the bottom,
And no one knows I've even got them.

Four hundred watts of halogen light;
Blueberry ladies dance through the night.
Some are heavy, and some are thin,
But these lovely girls sure make me grin.

A closet may hold many desires,
But I don't think I can get much higher;
With buds in a bag and a smile on my face,
This closet has become my favorite place.

Some may say I'm out of my mind,
But I can grow almost any kind
Of heavenly herb with just a seed,
And a secret garden is all that I need.

CHAPTER 7

A Secret Franchise for Indoor Growing

I'll tell you a secret that millionaires know:
Money on trees is easy to grow.

When I was selling real estate in Washington State back in the late '90s, I had a potential client come into my office looking for rural property, preferably deep in the woods and off the map. Normally I didn't taxi clients around, because I was too busy with my own schedule, but he was a cash buyer and he said that he would pay me a hundred dollars an hour for my time. After two weeks of searching the multiple listings, we found nothing that he was interested in. I thought it was best that we have lunch and rethink what we were doing. So, over Mexican food, he told me this story.

He said that he was the son of a scientist who was the director of research for a major pineapple company . Over the years, his father had developed a new technology for growing plants that doubled the crop production in a single year. Today they call it liquid fertilizer and hydroponics, but back then his research was still in the experimental stages of development. It was one of the most closely guarded secrets in the industrialized world because of the potential products that it would bring to the market in the future.

As a teenager, he started smoking marijuana and growing pot in a secluded field in back of his house, using his father's liquid fertilizer. The buds he grew were legendary among his friends. Then one day his father's company had an employee open-house party, and he got to see the laboratory that was using the new hydroponics growing system for growing baby pineapples indoors under lights. He took the idea to his uncle's house and started to experiment growing buds inside the garage using old street lights that he found in the junkyard. He eventually followed in his father's footsteps and graduated from college with a PhD in biology and chemistry. But instead of going to work for someone else, he decided to start his own indoor marijuana business and became the entrepreneur of his teenage dreams. His first customers were his friends and their fellow students at the university. Then he sold pounds to friends who sailed their own yachts back and forth between Hawaii and San Francisco. By the time he was twenty-four years old he was a millionaire.

After he made his second million, he decided to move to the mainland (because that's where the largest number of consumers are) and start a new indoor grow business, which he hoped he could franchise to other entrepreneurs eager to get into the cannabis industry. His business idea went something like this: He would finance the entire business, land, house, equipment, seeds, food, and a monthly salary, plus medical coverage in case the investor somehow got hurt. He would install and provide instructions for a completely automated indoor grow with the most technologically advanced equipment available. He would help harvest and package the product. He would transport and sell the product and pay the investor $2,000 in cash every month for the first two years. At the end of that time, the investor would have the opportunity to buy the business at fair market value, continue the business the way it was, or walk away and let someone else take over the opportunity. In return, the investor would have to agree to a strict code of conduct that may have seemed unreasonable to some people but to others more than fair (given the scope of the opportunity to become a millionaire within a relatively short period of time).

The Code of Conduct

1. Live alone on the property at all times.
2. Let no one else on the property at any time (including family, friends, or loved ones).
3. Only leave the property for supplies or medical reasons.

4. Learn how to operate and repair the equipment effectively, including the generators.
5. No drinking in public bars, restaurants, lounges, clubs, etc.
6. No smoking cigarettes on the property.
7. Pets limited to one outside dog and one cat.
8. All furniture, stereo, TV, computer, and appliances belong to the owner.
9. No hunting or discharging firearms on the property.
10. No loud music or outside noise.
11. No cable or satellite TV; no mail or UPS delivery (cell phone okay).
12. An agreement must be signed for no drug activity on the property.

Formula for a Professional Indoor Grow

A. Buy 20 acres in the country away from any neighbors.
B. Construct a full-size secret basement with a concealed outside entrance.
C. Conceal all electrical lines, plumbing lines, water lines, and the air ventilation system. Hook up a generator.
D. Have a concrete slab poured over the hidden basement.
E. Buy a modular home and have it delivered and installed on a foundation over the slab.
F. Live completely off the grid.
G. Grow your garden and rule yourself.

Pay attention, because this is how you can make a million dollars growing marijuana indoors. Inside your hidden basement, you'll need to build three separate rooms, each with their own solid door, electrical outlets, and a water faucet. Each room will need to be ventilated. The first room will be used as a nursery; that's where you'll propagate seeds or make clones from the mother plants. It doesn't have to be very big, maybe ten by twelve. You'll need four 5-foot fluorescent grow lights (sometimes called aquarium lights), two worktables, potting soil, 700 seeds, and grow cups. The second and third rooms will take up the remainder of the basement.

The second room will have ten 600-watt metal hi-lad lights (five on each side of the room). You'll need ten 22-gallon plastic containers with holes in the bottom, and four bricks for drainage under each container. Place one container with bricks on a flat furniture dolly for easy mobility. (Rotating the containers helps mimic sunlight, and the plants receive more light between the branches.) Fill each container with the best soil you can find, plant twenty seedlings per container, and place one container under each light. Program the lights for a twelve-hour-on and twelve-hour-off cycle until the plants are twelve to eighteen inches high (about six to eight weeks).

Then move the containers into the flowering room (or budding room), place each container under a 1,000-watt metal hi-lad light, and put them on a schedule of eighteen hours on and six hours off. This will make the plants start to flower, or bud, and this is also the time to remove male plants so the buds won't become "seeded" and bring you a poor price at the bargaining table. Plants will be ready to harvest about 120 days after they are planted, or when the white fibers on the buds turn red or light brown in color. While the plants are in the flowering stage, go back to the nursery and start more seedlings, then move them to the vegetation room, then move them into the flowering room, and then harvest. Repeat the process over again. The idea is to grow as many buds as you can under each 1,000-watt light. Hopefully you can harvest enough buds to make your dreams come true.

Using a modern-day indoor hydroponics growing system can be very complicated and expensive, and it's probably better if you start out using natural soil in containers until you have the time to learn about pumps, holding tanks, dials, and gauges, etc. However, learning the hydroponic indoor growing system has its advantages, because you can grow more buds in less time once you master the technique. This is always a good thing when you're trying to grow a million dollars' worth of plant material.

Professional Indoor Grow Formula
This is based on a 120-day grow cycle and a market value of $2,500 per pound of top-quality seedless dried buds.
There are three 120-day harvests in one year.
We are estimating one pound of dried buds times 10 lights.

10 lb. x $2,500 market value = $25,000 per harvest
$25,000 x 3 harvests = $75,000 tax-free per year
$75,000 x 10 years = $750,000 tax-free in 10 years

This may not quite be the million-dollar goal you're looking for, *but* try to wrap your entrepreneur skills around this idea and take it one step further. Subdivide the twenty acres into two ten-acre parcels; build two hidden basements and two homes. Double your income.

20 lb. x $2,500 market value = $50,000 per harvest
$50,000 x 3 harvests = $150,000 tax-free per year
$150,000 x 10 years = $1,500,000 tax-free in 10 years ($3 million tax-free in twenty years)

After twenty years of self-rule you can retire in luxury, *but* let's take this idea and expand it into another universe. Subdivide the twenty acres into four five-acre parcels, build a hidden basement and a house on each parcel, and quadruple your income. This is based on the principle that if you can grow one pound you can grow a hundred.

40 lb. x $2,500 market value = $100,000 per harvest
$100,000 x 3 harvests = $300,000 tax-free per year
$300,000 x 5 years = $1,500,000 tax-free in 5 years
$300,000 x 10 years = $3 million tax-free in 10 years ($6 million tax-free for 20 years' work!)

This formula can be franchised and sold on the free market, and it's a secret that the government and big business don't want you to know about. That's why they are spending billions of dollars demonizing the cannabis plant—because they don't want you to self-rule. But "they" are losing the war, and they know it. There are thousands, perhaps tens of thousands, of entrepreneurs in the cannabis industry who are pioneering this country into a new century, and nothing short of mass murder is going to stop *them*.

Meanwhile, back at the lunch table with my potential buyer who was looking for franchise property in eastern Washington. He was sharing with me how many franchise opportunities he had on the West Coast. He had four in California, two in Arizona, three in Oregon, and three on the west side of Washington State. He was asking me to help him find a good location somewhere north of Spokane. He wasn't bragging about how much money he was making, but a quick estimate in my head looked something like this:

12 grow sites, each making $100,000 yearly = $1.2 million tax-free a year
1.2 million x 5 years = $6 million tax-free

Even if he subtracted his cost for labor, equipment, fuel, and construction, etc., his profit would still be considerable, especially after five years. We didn't discuss some of the specifics of the business, such as how often he changed the soil in the containers, or what would happen if someone wanted to quit or got sick in the middle of harvesting. But I was curious about how he handled the transporting of the product and the cash. He said that he very rarely carried pounds and large amounts of cash at the same time. The pot was vacuum sealed and packed in coffee grounds hidden in a secret compartment underneath the backseat. Sometimes he would have a dog in back, and sometimes it would be covered with suitcases and clothes as if he were on a business trip. In all the years that he had been traveling, he had only been pulled over once for speeding, and the car was never searched. He told me that in every state where he was doing business he also owned a home in the country, so he wouldn't be driving more than a few hours at a time. Large amounts of money were also vacuum sealed and stored in the same secret compartment. He never kept more than fifty thousand dollars in his savings account and no more than twelve thousand dollars in his checking account. The bulk of his money was buried in different places on his property. He never made deposits of more than ten thousand dollars at a time, and if he bought something big, like a car or a house, he would make a small down payment and finance the rest over time. Then he would make five-thousand—or ten-thousand-dollar payments as soon as he could, to pay off the debt. Some of his money he used to buy small businesses, so he had a legitimate answer if anyone asked him what he did for a living. He owned a self-serve car wash, two Laundromats, and a Dairy

Queen, and had a payroll of six employees. But his family admired him the most for his partnership in a popular real-estate franchise in downtown Seattle. He had never been audited, but if he were, his lawyers would handle the details.

After lunch, he said that there was something in his car that he wanted to show me, so we went to the parking lot and got in the front seat of his car. From the glove compartment he took out a brown envelope with twenty pictures. He explained that every year he threw a party for all his franchise holders, and he would rent a suite in one of the best hotels in Las Vegas. Everything would be gratis, including some of the finest and most beautiful women in the world. The photos showed people enjoying themselves in every conceivable sexual activity imaginable from the waist up. If I looked past the nipples and beards, I could see buffet tables with food and champagne spread out in front of windows with views of the Vegas skyline. Each grower brought with him a sample of his crops, and there were photos of cigar boxes full the finest looking buds money could grow. Everyone was too busy to worry about who was taking the pictures, but nevertheless, it looked like a great party with the growers celebrating the success of another profitable harvest.

This was one of the most interesting people I had ever met, and he was doing exactly what I wanted to do. I wished that I could have taken him up on his franchise opportunity, *but* I was a married man with a real-estate license hanging around my neck, and I was too old and too scared to take the chance. However, about two years later, I did sell him a beautiful home on a hundred acres between Spokane and Coeur d'Alene, Idaho. It was a new home, built by a contractor who was looking to retire in the woods and live completely off the grid, away from the crazy world. He had been killed in a motorcycle accident not long after the house was built.

I often think about that entrepreneur in the cannabis industry who was creating the opportunity for American citizens to stand up on their own two feet and take back their lives, take back their country, and take back their freedom of choice—to decide whether they want to rule themselves or wanted the government to tell them how to live their lives.

I decided for myself that when I retired I was going to have my own secret garden and use the buds to supplement my income, because I knew deep in my heart that the thieves in the White House had already stolen my Social Security check and were trying to steal the American dream too.

Money on Trees

By Chuck Allen Jr.

I'll tell you a secret that millionaires know:
Money on trees is easy to grow.
They pick it like fruit and dry it on racks;
Follow the money, and you'll learn the facts.

Seclusion and water, with plenty of light
Will make you a fortune, even at night.
A few tiny seeds can produce a spark,
Bright as the sun in a basement dark.

A large tree of fiber, a small tree of herbs,
Lose their meaning with a war on words.
I'll tell you the difference between fuel and health:
Money on trees can spread the wealth.

Supply and demand is the name of the game;
Consumption and production are not the same thing.
Find a good product that will help fill a niche,
And the pursuit of happiness will make you rich.

CHAPTER 8

A Secret Desert Grow Story

When the Indians were given the worst possible land,
A place full of misery and burning hot sand,
They built their casinos, turning straw into gold,
And bought back the freedom their ancestors sold.

I was living in Arizona, in the spring of 2002, six months after the Twin Towers in New City were destroyed by Muslim extremists. I was sitting at the counter in a local restaurant, eating pancakes and reading the morning paper, when a hard-looking woman came in and took the seat next to me at the counter. Her hair was pulled back in a ponytail, with loose strands sticking out like electrified spaghetti. The skin on her face was wrinkled and dark from too many years in the desert sun. She was wearing three turquoise rings on each hand that looked to be authentic Indian jewelry.

If I had to guess her age, I would say she was probably in her late '50s or '60s, give or take a few generations. When her coffee came, she emptied about a third of the sugar bowl into her cup, stirred it with a fork for two minutes, and then poured coffee into the saucer and started slurping the goodness from out of the air. It was a strange and exotic sound, loud enough to gain the attention of the cook standing in the kitchen thirty feet away. With her elbows on the counter and both little fingers sticking out from the saucer, she looked like Kokopelli on Prozac. After she finally put the coffee down and tapped her lips with the paper napkin, she turned to me and whispered, "Confucius say, 'Woman who stands on toilet is high on pot.'" It was all I could do to keep from spewing my mouthful of pancakes all over the newspaper in front of my face. It was not what I was expecting to hear from an old woman who had just come in from the desert heat. I couldn't stop the grin from creeping across the front of my beard, but before I could say a word, I caught a glimpse of the waitress shaking her head—no, no—and talking with her hands, saying, "Please don't encourage her anymore!" It was then that I caught a whiff of the aroma coming from her clothes. It was the unmistakable smell of what the nose knows, *Cannabis sativa*, blended with desert sage.

I was a closet pot smoker myself, so I couldn't help but admire her spunk and tenacity—but not in a restaurant full of people. So I told her that she sounded like a very interesting person, and I asked if we couldn't continue the conversation at the park down by the river. She told me that she loved that place and that she would meet me there in ten minutes.

I was a happily married man, and I wasn't interested in her in a sexual way, but pot smokers are a different type of human being, and they are often very intellectual and creative when it comes to the subject of marijuana. They know more about it than some people who say they do when they really don't. I just found it interesting that she seemed to be so carefree and open about anything, and I was so careful and conservative about everything.

The southern part of the Colorado River snakes its way between Nevada, Arizona, and California, supplying the region with an abundance of clear, cold water. As we sat on a concrete bench watching the river flow from right to left, the contrast between the dry, barren banks and the sunlight dancing on the translucent waterway set the stage for our conversation. She told me her name was Nancy and that it really didn't fit in with her Indian last name, Mountain Walker, but she decided to keep it anyway. I told her that my name was Alan, but it really didn't fit in with my last name, Charles, and we laughed. I said that I had a hard time explaining to my family in Kansas how clear the Colorado River was because they only knew the ugly, stinking, muddy Missouri River. She said that people are limited by what they don't know. Then she took a puff and passed me a joint. I took a puff and passed it back. I said that they had taken history out of the schools and now the kids didn't know the difference between a republic and democracy. She took a puff and passed it to me. She said that they had been doing that to the Indians for a hundred years. I took a puff and passed it back. I said that the Indians still had their sovereignty and we didn't. We laughed and put the joint out; we both had had enough. I told her that I now understood why her last name was Mountain Walker, and she laughed longer than I did. For the next year or so, we talked about all the different kinds of pot we had smoked and eventually got around to the topic of which was the best, marijuana grown indoors or outdoors. I said that the best I ever had was grown in the hills of northern California, and she said the best pot in the world was grown in the Nevada desert. I said that it was too hot and that marijuana didn't do well in temperatures over 80 degrees. She said that she wasn't talking about growing in the desert but under the desert.

Nancy asked me to take a look at the land across the river. She told me that the government had given the Indians 180,000 acres to live on forever and ever. On the surface it sounded generous, but underneath it was the worst land in America, good for growing nothing but casinos and alcoholism. Sure, the tribal council leased out some land along the river with irrigation rights, but generally speaking, Indians weren't farmers. They contracted out the bulk of the work to farmers from the south, who knew what they doing, how to repair and operate the farming equipment and rotate the crops. She said that if I had a few hours to spare, she would like to show me some Indian farming techniques that few white men would ever get to see. It was my day off, and my wife was at work, so I didn't see any harm in taking a tour of the reservation.

We got in her truck, drove across the river, and headed into the desert on one of those long, dusty roads that seem to go on forever. After about five miles, we turned onto an access road that was nothing but tire tracks in the sand, beaten down over time into a narrow trail that zigzagged over and around low hills and came to a stop in front of a single-wide mobile home. She turned the truck off, and we got out. I could barely hear a generator somewhere in the distance. I helped her unload four cans of gasoline and five cans of water and store them in the shade under the front porch. I was starting to get the picture now; she must have a closet grow somewhere in the back of the trailer. I was expecting the house to be stiffening hot, but it wasn't. We were greeted by a refreshing current of air that was cooled by an old-fashioned window air conditioner with water flowing over filters. It wasn't the best system on the market, but it was easy to maintain and good enough to make desert living enjoyable.

Nancy was a collector. Every square inch of her small home was filled with objects of desire, various works of art, and knickknacks to which she must have attached some importance. There was a narrow path from the kitchen to the bedroom with barely enough room to turn around. I couldn't see any trash anywhere; there were no newspapers, magazines, or dirty dishes in the sink. The bathroom was small but clean, and the bedroom had a single bed with a sleeping bag and a pillow. There was at least one mirror on every wall, giving the impression of windows with views where there were none. There was one small round table in the kitchen, with two chairs, no couch, no TV, and no radio. There was a small refrigerator in the corner, and a .22 revolver with a box of shells sitting on the kitchen counter, giving the impression of peace and security. A small oil lamp stood on the table and a single stack of paperbacks on the floor. All in all, the place seemed comfortable for an eccentric old woman living by herself in the middle of the desert.

I saw no signs of marijuana or paraphernalia anywhere in the house, but there was a wooden cigar box next to the toaster; it wouldn't take tea with Sherlock Homes to figure that one out. Also, I couldn't smell the aroma of buds, if they were being grown inside such a small space.

I understood now why she came into the restaurant and interrupted my breakfast. She was starved for attention and needed someone to talk to. But I didn't really mind; most of her opinions made more sense than those of any journalist working for the mass media.

The first thing she wanted to show me was her "power station" (two generators, one for backup). They were hidden about a hundred yards from the trailer inside a concrete bunker. This was open on both ends for air circulation, and it had a wooden roof to help the generator keep cool. The electrical line was pulled through a two-inch PVC pipe and buried in the sand. I saw three 5-gallon plastic gas cans resting in the shade of a camouflage tarpaulin nearby. As we were walking back to the house, Nancy suddenly stopped and asked me whether I could see anything unusual in her backyard. I knew this was a trick question, but I didn't have an answer. All I could see was a few low hills, covered with the usual desert rocks, cactus, and sticker bushes. The only thing out of the ordinary was a firepit with two benches under the blue sky. I know the sun was high, and so was I, but with the way the heat waves were rising up from the sand and the sweat dripping from my brow I swear Nancy turned into Kokopelli again and started dancing around the firepit playing her lucky air flute with her fingers. When she stopped, she shuffled over to one of the benches and tipped it over, revealing a hidden ladder welded to the inside of a galvanized culvert pipe big enough for a large man to climb into. There was a lightbulb on the wall next to a wooden door at the bottom of the ladder. Nancy stood there, nervously looking around as if someone could be watching, and then she started telling me this story. She said that her father worked in the construction industry, and one weekend he had brought home a backhoe and dug out the side of a hill, a large enough hole to bury a metal container about the size of a Safeway truck. The electrical line, water line, and ventilation system were all hidden underground. The room at the bottom of the stairs was the nursery, with two fluorescent grow lights; the middle room was the grow room, with six 400-watt lights; and the end room was the blooming room, with eight 1,000-watt lights. The joint we had tasted earlier in the day had come from this grow.

In the nursery there was a small couch, a table with one chair, and a portable stereo in the comer. On the walls were framed color photographs of various buds that had been grown in her secret garden. In the second room were four hundred healthy plants about eighteen inches tall. In the last room were two hundred 3-gallon plants, with buds as long as my forearm, all standing straight and tall. I didn't know who this woman was, but she was accomplishing more than I ever had with my closet grows. As she took me from room to room, explaining her process of growing, I couldn't help but think that this size garden would be perfect for the average entrepreneur, because it wasn't so big as to attract attention, and yet it was large enough to bring in a decent income from taking a risk.

I never came out and asked her how much she was making, but I would guess somewhere around $25,000 tax-free a year. Not bad for a little old lady in her retirement years. So, let's do some math real quick. My guess is that Nancy was growing four pounds of dried buds every four months (120 days, three times a year).

4 lb. x $2,000 bulk value = $8,000 every 4 months
3 crops x $8,000 = $24,000 tax-free a year
$24,000 x 10 years = $240,000 tax-free to retire on

If she were getting $2,500 bulk value for her buds, the formula would look different.
4 lb. x $2,500 bulk value = $10,000 every 4 months
3 crops x $10,000 = $30,000 tax-free a year
$30,000 x 10 years = $300,000 tax-free to retire on

Still not a million dollars but more than enough to live comfortably on in her later years.

Nancy explained to me that living on the reservation was like living in a foreign country. The Indians are a sovereign nation, which means that they aren't ruled by another government, with the exception of federal laws. But when it comes to growing marijuana on Indian land, the government considers it a state or local problem that should be handled by the local tribal councils. And most tribal members believe that marijuana is a traditional herbal medicine that should be honored and respected, not demonized as by the white man. Also the Indians believe that marijuana is a much better choice for self-medication than alcohol or prescription drugs. The white man is always declaring war on something, but they are foolish to declare war on a beneficial plant.

Nancy had found herself a business partner without even trying; all she had to do was take a pound over to her friend's house and drop it off and then come back in a few weeks and pick up the money. Her indoor garden was allowing two people to rule themselves and contribute to the economy by using the money to consume goods and services they otherwise couldn't afford.

Meanwhile, back at Nancy's house in the desert, it was close to 4 o'clock in the afternoon, and I needed to get back so I could pick my wife up from work. But Nancy said that she wanted to show me one last indoor growing business that no white man had ever seen before and lived to tell about. I told her that I didn't want to get into something that I couldn't get out of, and she laughed and said for me not to worry, because I was with the Mountain Walker. She said that it was only going to take us ten minutes to get there, and all we were going to do was park on a hill and look down on a small Indian village

About eight miles southeast of her house, we pulled over and stopped on the side of a road overlooking a community of double-wide manufactured homes. Each appeared to have a different floor plan, and they looked modern. The streets were paved and clean. The yards were green and trim, with fenced-in backyards. There were no busted windows, junk cars, or broken appliances littering the properties. I could see a school, a grocery store, and a gas station. There were some official brick buildings that looked like those for medical services, or a fire department, or maybe a water department. These reservation homes looked nothing like what I had seen in California or Washington State; those had resembled inner-city government housing projects, with abandoned buildings and broken spirits.

Nancy explained to me that there were five tribal families growing marijuana in the basements of their homes and selling the buds through their connections in the casinos around the area. The money that they were generating was improving the quality of their lives and giving them back the courage and self-respect that had been destroyed by the white man's progressive movement across their land. Their secret gardens were equipped with the best growing systems that money could buy, and the Indians had become experts in the field of hydroponic gardening. Their seed propagation was producing the best marijuana in the world, and the stupid white consumers were thinking that the buds were coming from Amsterdam or Canada. These independent small businesses were giving back to the Indian people their pride and dignity and the ability to rule themselves without government handouts or the tribal council permission.

It's true that not all Indians are entrepreneurs, just as not all white people are businessmen. But there are enough of them now who are making a positive difference in the Indian nation, and they don't have to accept some twisted form of social democracy controlled by a consorted group of rich people who have an agenda that goes far beyond "one nation under God."

Nancy turned the truck around, and we returned to her house in the desert. We remained friends for many years after that day, and my wife and I enjoyed some of our favorite memories sitting around that firepit under those magnificent desert stars, smoking the peace pipe with Kokopelli and her herbal friends.

The American Indian

By Chuck Allen Jr.

Long before Columbus decided to roam,
The Indians made this land their home.
They knew about the white man even before
A foreign ship came to this shore.

From top of the mountain to down on the plains,
Plants and animals were given their names.
The spirit of the ancestors lived in the smoke,
Passed in a circle, so everyone could toke.

Tobacco grew wild in the fields and meadows,
While birds planted seeds, where ganja grows.
When he mixed it in bowl and placed it in pipe,
The shaman discovered a medical delight.

Then along came the pioneers, looking to settle;
In the Indian's life they would constantly meddle.
And when push came to shove, at the Indian's cost,
It was the white man's soul that was finally lost.

When the Indians were given the worst possible land,
A place full of misery and burning hot sand,
They built their casinos, turning straw into gold,
And bought back the freedom their ancestors sold.

Today when the drum beats at the ceremonial dance,
The children of the ancestors will be given a chance
To choose for themselves the way of the smoke
And pass the pipe in a circle for everyone to toke.

CHAPTER 9

The Secret Life of a Fireman's Wife

The forest can grow an abundance of things;
It's a shame to lose them to smoke and flames.

This story was told to me by a woman who wished to remain anonymous. It's a story about her, her husband, and their son, who were farming cannabis in the county of Mendocino back in the mid to late '80s. She told me this story at her home in Santa Rosa, California, a few months before she died. She was a longtime friend and college classmate. I admired her and her family for their courage and determination to stand on their principles and rule themselves.

Back in the late '80s, she opened a video store inside a supermarket in a small town in California. She knew that it sounded crazy, but she had something else in mind to sell besides videos. Anyway, when the grocery shoppers entered the store, they would be greeted by a wide stairway that presented them with a choice: either they went up the stairs to her little shop, or they went around the stairway to find the grocery store. The new owners couldn't think of one reason why customers would climb all those stairs to shop for groceries, not for the bakery or meat departments, and certainly not for the wine and liquor department. It wasn't a good idea to have drunks navigating all those steps, but the insurance company didn't have a problem with a video store, so she signed a two-year lease. Hell, drunks and potheads had been crashing and burning on the stairway to heaven for thousands of years—what's a few more steps in a video store?

She called her business Show Time Video, and people seemed to like it. They could go shopping and pick up a video at the same time, and then return it the next time they were hungry. Thank goodness the owners of the building only charged her a small monthly fee, because her profit margin selling videos was about 3 percent. She thought they rented her the space more for the public relations than for anything else.

Her biggest selling item in the store wasn't videos; it was the small bags of marijuana she sold from behind the counter. She could honestly say from experience that there are more pot smokers in our society than you can possibly imagine. One of the most interesting things she found out about the cannabis industry is the don't-ask-don't-tell honor system between the growers and the consumers. The whole cannabis industry depends upon it. The reason our legal system is poisoned and corrupt is because there is no presumption of innocence until proven guilty. In reality, a person is presumed guilty until proven innocent, because that's the way the court system works. Why should the courts presume anything? A person gets caught, gets arrested, and has a trial. There is no presumption of innocence. They go through the system, and they are either released or incarcerated. Why should there be a presumption of anything? The presumption of innocence is only symbolic and is not found in the Constitution. It's the legal pundits who have found a way to foul the system by using symbolism to create delays and confusion in order to make more money for themselves and/or their clients.

The cannabis industry works on a much more honest and truthful symbolic system: "Ask if it's true, and don't tell if it is." The social network of marijuana consumers in our culture runs deep and wide, and they aren't interested in the government or big business helping them achieve social justice. The free marketplace, with its own supply and demand, is strong and healthy and doesn't need the help of lawyers and judges to continue to exist one way or the other. Small marijuana businesses like the one she had will continue to grow and survive because of the supply and demand of the American consumer, in spite of the government's war on drugs and on the citizens who use them. Those are the reasons she sold pot. Now for the rest of the story.

Did all the residents of this small town know she was selling pot? Maybe, maybe not. Did all the pot smokers know? Maybe, maybe not. She was sure most of them did, but so what? As long as they were adults and pursuing their own happiness, where was the crime and who was the victim? She never sold to someone who wasn't twenty-one or who she didn't know, and she never kept more than an ounce in the store at one time.

She only sold one or two 1/8-ounce packages of buds at a time. Normally, the consumer can roll four or five joints (maybe more, maybe less, depending on how big the joints are). One 1/8-ounce bag, smoked in a bong or a pipe, could last two or three weeks, maybe a month, but someone who parties a lot could go through a 1/8-ounce bag in a matter of hours.

If she sold one bag for $40, that would calculate to $320 per ounce (8 bags x $40 = $320). If she made $320 a day, that would come out to $1,600 a week, or $6,400 tax-free a month. Multiply that by twelve, and the profit is $76,800. If she kept the business for ten years, she could make $760,800 tax-free. Not a million dollars, but better than government work. Her formula for success looked like this:

$320 x 5 days = $1,600 tax-free a week
$1,600 x 4 weeks = $6,400 tax-free a month
$6,400 x 12 months = $76,800 tax-free a year
$76,800 x 10 years = $760,800 tax-free

If one pound cost me $2,000, and I sold 128 bags for $40 each, I would make $5,120.
$5,120—$2,000 = $3,120 tax-free

If I sold two pounds a month, the formula would look like this:

$10,240—$4,000 = $6,240 tax-free

She knew that all this pot business sounded complicated and dangerous but it really wasn't. It was like riding a roller coaster at the amusement park; once you get comfortable in the seat, the ride takes care of itself. If you don't like roller coasters, don't get in.

Her husband and her son were very successful pot growers between 1980 and 1985. They lived in a small town with a population of two thousand people. Her husband was the fire chief and their son was a deputy sheriff working Highway 5 up and down central California. Everyone knew who they were but didn't have a clue about their secret gardens.

Her son first got the idea of starting his own pot business when he saw up close and personal how hopeless the war on drugs truly was. He had smoked pot from high school through college and had friends in the sheriff's department who casually smoked pot too, and they all knew that marijuana wasn't the Frankenstein's monster that the villagers should be scared of. He saw the war on marijuana from every side imaginable—from the thieves who were shot dead because they were too lazy to grow their own to the DEA agents proudly having their pictures taken in front of tons of marijuana being burned instead of being donated to health-care providers for patients who needed it for medical purposes. In all those cases, it wasn't the marijuana that was the problem; it was the corrupt system that was out of control.

When her husband and son went on camping trips together, they would sit around the fire and pass the pipe and sip a few beers; it was as natural as the stars twinkling in the sky. Both of them had stressful, dangerous jobs, and on any given day they knew it could be their last on earth. Marijuana for them, and millions of other hardworking people, relieved the stress and anxiety of a hostile environment caused by a government that was trying to control every aspect of their lives. Using marijuana was a way for them to help understand the difficult and complex problems our politicians were creating for the American people. While we were putting our faith and confidence in them by electing them to public office, they were stealing our Social Security checks and paying communists and socialists to teach our children.

What her husband found so wrong about the system was the idea that public land belonged exclusively to politicians, not the taxpayers who had paid for the land in the first place. As fire chief, it was part of his responsibility to guard and protect the public lands surrounding his small community. There were tens of thousands of acres of public land that the average citizen couldn't use because of the so-called fire danger. The access roads were kept locked, and it was his job to help make sure the taxpaying public stayed out. What most people don't understand is that more fires are caused by lightning strikes and downed power lines than by campfires, cigarettes, and matches. Elected officials use public land as their own private playgrounds, whereas the average citizen can't.

Lawyers, judges, mayors, and any number of self-proclaimed important people would abuse the system by calling the fire chief's office and asking for a certain gate to be unlocked so they could go fishing, camping, or hiking with their family, friends, or business associates. Consequently, this woman's husband felt a great injustice was being served against the American people, and that's why he saw no reason not to use the land to make money to give back to the community what their leaders were taking from them. After all, the land belonged to the taxpayers.

So her husband and son used the keys kept at the fire department to let themselves into state land, where they grew many pounds of marijuana. They had aerial maps of where water was located (springs, ponds, streams, and lakes), and they found the best places to grow. They planted four different gardens in May and harvested in late September. She never went with them and didn't know how big the gardens were, but she heard them talking about it many times, and she was sure that they harvested at least four hundred pounds every year for ten years (two hundred pounds dried).

They always made sure she had a pound for the video store each month, and her son would keep twelve pounds for himself. The rest of the crop was bought by a professor from Oakland, California, and a real estate broker from San Francisco. The bulk of their money was packaged in ziplock freezer bags and stored in thirty-gallon plastic garbage cans buried on their property in the country. She never met the buyers, but she heard talk about the market price of marijuana all the time, and apparently the market price of pounds changed from crop to crop, but generally speaking pounds would sell for $2,000 to $2,500. She often tried to figure out how much money they were making, and her guess was about half a million a year.

200 lb. x $2,500 = $500,000
$500,000 x 10 years = $5 million tax-free

All she knew for sure was that they had made a lot of money in a short period of time, and their lives and those around them were greatly enriched because of their efforts. They invested in their community by opening a public food bank for emergencies and a free soup kitchen for anyone who was hungry, building an art gallery for local artists, and starting a public-transportation service and a home-delivery business for senior citizens.

The cannabis industry had been very good to her family; it had enabled them to contribute significantly not only to the quality of their own lives but also to the economy of a free country. This demonstrated to the whole world that the cannabis plant wasn't the monster that our leaders pretended it to be and that it wasn't corrupting the moral fiber of the country. On the contrary, it was enabling them to grow a stronger moral fiber, which was bonding this nation with its people.

The most important thing about the cannabis industry that everyone needs to remember is that it's producing the soldiers who are protecting this republic. This family strongly encouraged anyone who had the courage and determination to make a living in the cannabis industry to do so. They are the pioneers of the future. Hopefully, one day soon this nation of "sheeple" will realize more fully that men and women can rule *themselves*.

A Firefighter's New Life

By Chuck Allen Jr.

When I was a young firefighter in 1963,
I found myself working in a secluded valley.
The day was hot, my throat was dry,
Yellow-red smoke filled the afternoon sky.
I stopped for a moment to take a drink;
Ash and smoke were making me blink.
My buddies were working south of the creek;
I was standing on a hill that was long and steep.
I put down the shovel and dropped my pack;
My eye caught something as I took off my hat.
A bird-net fence, from tree to tree,
Stretched down the hill as far as I could see.
Inside the fence was a sea of green,
The biggest pot garden I have ever seen.
What could I do? What could I say?
What if the fire kept burning this way?
A fortune was waiting for me to pick;
How to harvest it was really the trick.
Without being caught, without being seen,
How could I keep this sea of green?
I sprang into action, with a moment to choose;
All of those buds I just couldn't lose.
Fifty holes with full-grown plants
Was worth the effort, was worth the chance.
I could hear my buddies call out my name,
But harvesting those buds was really the game.
I yelled down the valley that all was okay,
I would see them again at the end of the day.
My worry right then was to beat the flames;
To lose all those buds would be a shame.
In an hour or two, I managed to cut
All of the plants, with a little luck.
I buried my dream in the side of that hill,

Hoping the flames would bypass them still.
I picked up my shovel and ran with my pack,
Sliding down that hill with smoke at my back.
I never felt guilty about finding that garden;
A whole new life this firefighter was starting.
The forest can grow an abundance of things;
It's a shame to lose them to smoke and flames.

CHAPTER 10

The Secret Story of the Hemp Boutique

Back in the days when hemp was king,
The value of the fiber was everything.

This story was told to me by a good friend who was the CEO of a major insurance company in Florida. He wrote a book about it but never had it published. I asked him whether I could tell his story in this book, and he agreed, but only if I changed the names and locations to protect freedom. It's based on his business adventure that challenges the foundation of the free-market system.

In the spring of 1982, my wife and I opened our first hemp boutique in the Santa Rosa Mall, and we named it The Ragged Sailor's Adventure. It was an upscale boutique that sold exclusive hemp products, which we imported from around the world. We commissioned manufacturers of hemp products to provide exclusive, hard-to-find items that people could buy only in our store.

When the customer walked into the boutique, they walked into an ambience that was strictly exotic. On three walls were painted beautiful panoramic murals of three ancient sailing vessels on the waters of a mysterious river. In the background were pyramids covered with lush jungle vegetation and strangely different animals following the boats along the riverbank. Every piece of furniture in the store was made from hemp, including the carpet, the ceiling fans, and the dressing-room curtains. Even the paint on the walls and ceiling was made from hempseed oil. Nowhere inside the boutique could a customer find a symbol or picture of a marijuana plant; there were no words and no pot logos of any kind. None of our brochures or advertisements mentioned marijuana, and our employees were trained not to use the word when talking about our products. We had to educate the public and ourselves about the history and benefits of the cannabis plant because of all the propaganda and misinformation that has been taught in our schools and in the mass media. We actually had people tell us they were afraid to take a hemp product home because their teenagers might try to smoke it.

My wife designed a beautiful logo that was sewn, stamped, or engraved on all our products. This logo was a round picture of a red sailboat with white sails, floating on blue water. The sky was a golden yellow, with a green sun. Around the top and bottom were the words "The Ragged Sailor's Adventures."

Women flocked to our ladies' department to find aromatherapy mists, candles, massage oils, perfumes, hair conditioner, lip balms, skin lotions, salves, shampoo, soaps, bathrobes, dresses, swimsuits, and lingerie—all made from the finest hemp fabric and oils.

In the men's department, there was a huge selection of suits, shirts, pants, shoes, socks, sweaters, shorts, jackets, and a wide range of shampoos and colognes, all made from hemp or hemp by-products.

Our most popular items for both men and women were our signature Ragged Sailor jeans and T-shirts. They were so popular that we could hardly keep them on the shelves.

In the accessories department, we had the most complete selection of hosiery, purses, hats, wallets, handkerchiefs, scarves, and shawls found anywhere in northern California. We also sold watch bands, belts, gloves, luggage, briefcases, and jewelry. This was just a short list of the items manufactured from the hemp plant.

Our sporting-goods department displayed some of the most durable tents, sleeping bags, coats, and boots that money could buy. Hemp backpacks, duffel bags, and travel kits were also very popular.

In the furniture department, we had the most wonderful handcrafted hemp headboards, bed frames, coffee tables, dining-room tables, cabinets, dressers, and end tables. Customers were particularly excited about our hemp mattresses and futons with matching sheets and pillowcases.

In our first year of being in business, we made a net profit of $720,670 with gross sales of $2.5 million. In our second year of operation, we opened our first fast-food restaurant in the mall food court, named The Ragged Sailor On the Go. Food items on the menu were created entirely from hemp oils, seed meal, and by-products—and the food was popular beyond our wildest dreams. Not only was the food delicious, it was nutritious as well: rich in omega-3s and heart-healthy ingredients. Our best-selling items were the flame-grilled burgers with fries and the fresh-made pizzas, sold in single, double, or family sizes. The burgers were made from spiced hemp seed meal, hemp seed oil, and salt and pepper. The buns were baked from de-fatted and de-hulled hemp seed flour and topped with hemp seeds instead of sesame seeds.

The fries were made from fresh-ground hemp seed meal mixed with milk and salt and then molded to look like French fries—but they tasted better because they were baked instead of fried. When the entire burger was put together with lettuce, tomato, onion, and the Ragged Sailor's secret sauce (ketchup, mayonnaise, and hemp oil), it became a delicious hot meal that everyone enjoyed.

The pizza dough was made from de-fatted and de-hulled hemp seed flour, which made a wonderful thin-crust pizza when mixed with spiced hemp seed oil and water. The dough could then be baked with the customers' favorite toppings and, of course, our famous cheeses made from hemp seed extract.

We served cold and hot drinks, cookies and chips, cake and ice cream, and energy bars—all made from hemp ingredients. One of our favorite desserts was a fruit-flavored lollipop made from hemp seed extract and natural sweeteners.

The restaurant's menu of ingredients and nutritional facts were posted so the public could compare the ingredients between our food and the major competitors'. We don't know exactly how it happened, but the Ragged Sailor's food to go became a phenomenon overnight, with nothing but word of mouth advertising.

All the hemp products sold in our restaurant were manufactured in other countries and imported into the United States for the American consumers. We consume more hemp products than any other country in the world, but the hemp industry is illegal in the United States. Does that make any sense to a normal businessman?

Why are we allowed to openly consume products in this country that are banned from being manufactured by our own people? I think our government wants to destroy the free enterprise system and the free marketplace to promote a new world order of Social Democracy—which is nothing but a code name for communism. Don't take my word for it; do your own research and open your own eyes. Then read the rest of this story and ask yourself just one question: *Why have the leaders of our country become the worst negotiators in the world?* You're probably thinking to yourself that hemp food doesn't sound very appetizing, but once you taste it you'll change your mind. The same thing happened when the hot dog first hit the marketplace; people didn't know what they were eating (most people still don't). They didn't understand that after a cow was butchered all the scraps and bits and pieces that were left over (including the ears, nose, lips, and eyeballs) were all ground together into one big vat and then the whole bloody mess was molded into the shape of a penis. Then they took some bread dough and molded it into the shape of a vagina. Then they placed the hot dog in the bun and sold it on the street corner, creating a billion-dollar industry. If the American consumer will eat that, they'll eat anything.

People have been eating hemp food in various recipes for thousands of years, but because of the war on drugs here in this country most people still think that eating hemp food will get them high. It wasn't until our restaurant opened in the mall that masses of people learned the truth and started to question what our government was doing with their war on the hemp plant.

At the end of our first year, The Ragged Sailor restaurant was averaging $27,000 a week, and it grossed $1.4 million. After expenses, we earned $463,320 in profits. Not bad for a business that was getting mixed reviews from critics who didn't understand what hemp seeds were and through their stupidity were perpetuating false rumors and lies in the media. We had to educate our competitors and customers every step of the way, and at times we felt a little overwhelmed at the ignorance of the American consumer.

My wife managed the boutique, and I managed the restaurant, and with her new line of hemp sweaters and waterproof jackets, and my new line of hemp wine-and-cheese products, our businesses were creating a new, more mature customer base that increased our business 5 percent in one month. Then we introduced a new gift catalog for both businesses, and we had to hire a security company to monitor the long lines. The only real problem we were having was with customers bringing food and drinks into the boutique and staining the merchandise and carpet while they were shopping. That problem was causing a considerable loss in profits after cleanup and repairs, but the overall mood of the crowds was enthusiastic and happy, with customer satisfaction at an all-time high (so to speak).

Local media stations were beginning to take notice of our popularity, and we had to instruct the staff not to talk to reporters without permission from the owners. Not that we had anything to hide; we just wanted to create an atmosphere of mystery and intrigue, because people are drawn to that kind of attitude whether they are rich or not.

It only took us three years to discover that the everyday stress and strain of running two successful businesses wasn't doing our marriage any good, so we decided to take a vacation. Our financial situation was improving, and we needed a break from all the headaches that we were creating. So we promoted a few key employees and booked a luxury cruise to Thailand, hoping to visit a number of countries that were manufacturing hemp products. We were still dumbfounded that the American businessmen couldn't recognize a good business opportunity if it jumped up and hit them right between the eyes.

In Thailand we found a hemp merchant who was eager to establish a good working relationship with an American businessman. We commissioned his company to manufacture, exclusively for the Ragged Sailor Corporation, a variety of specialty items like sports equipment, and accessories such as Frisbees, Hacky Sacks, skateboards, snowboards, and surfboards. We also commissioned ten thousand replicas of the original colonial flag, made from hemp fabric, and ten thousand replicas of the original Declaration of Independence, made from hemp paper, just like the original document. Both items were enclosed in glass, with a hemp frame. On the bottom of the frames was a brass plate explaining that the flag and the document were made from 100 percent hemp material. They would make a wonderful gifts for any person proud to be an American.

When we got back from our vacation, we contented ourselves by doing as little work as possible. In the mornings, we went from the boutique to the restaurant, checking paperwork and making bank deposits. In the afternoons, we sometimes would dress up as the Ragged Sailor and his first mate, to delight the customers and kids. We took the opportunity to pass out coupons for complimentary gifts for customers with birthdays.

On the Fourth of July weekend in 1985, both of our businesses in the mall were raided by the DEA, FBI, Sonoma County Sheriff's Office, and the Santa Rosa Police Department. There were thousands of holiday shoppers who witnessed the spectacular show of force. In a matter of moments the mall was surrounded, and teams of storm troopers ascended the escalators and entered both stores with automatic weapons drawn. Customers were pushed back into the hallways and forced to leave the building. My wife and I were arrested without explanation and taken away in handcuffs. There were news reporters with cameras and microphones waiting for us outside the building. Obviously they knew about the arrest before we did. We were placed in separate vehicles and taken to the FBI building in downtown San Francisco. Somewhere along the way, they read me my rights. When I asked them what the problem was, they said it had something to do with drugs or the possession of drugs or something like that; I was too confused and frightened to understand much of anything else. They took us into the FBI building through the back door, which was heavily guarded. Within the first hour we went through all the procedures any criminal would be expected to endure: mug shots, fingerprints, strip search, and the customary change of clothes. All of my identification, jewelry, and money was placed in a brown envelope and sealed with the same number that was stenciled on the front pocket of my orange jumpsuit.

Needless to say, I was made to feel like a criminal. I knew in my heart that this must be a huge mistake, unless one of our employees was dealing drugs, but how would we know about that? I felt certain that it had nothing to do with our business. All that propaganda you see on TV about getting a phone call doesn't apply when you're arrested by the FBI; they can do whatever they want to. They are very much like the IRS in that regard—lawless.

The next morning I had a breakfast of scrambled eggs, bacon, hash browns, toast, coffee, and a container of orange juice. The food was acceptable, but the situation wasn't. I was starting to get angry, but there wasn't anything I could do about it. I was helpless unless someone came to my rescue, and that didn't look like it was going to happen anytime soon. Later on that same morning, I was escorted in handcuffs to the office of the Director of Criminal Investigation. The name on the door said James P. Wright, but I was praying that he was totally wrong. I was nudged toward a leather chair in front of a large oak desk that was much bigger than the frail-looking man on the other side. He looked at me over the top of his tortoiseshell glasses and, without introduction, got right to the point.

He said that they had been watching me and my wife, for over three years, dealing with cannabis products that were imported into the United States for sale to the general public. He said, "Recently you returned from Thailand with a commercial container filled with cannabis products specifically manufactured for your upscale boutique located in the Santa Rosa Mall. They recently searched this container and found two hundred pounds of cannabis seeds illegally brought into this country. Unfortunately you may or may not realize this, but cannabis seeds are against the law in the United States. They can't be bought or distributed in this country. Now, we understand that there are items on your restaurant menu that are made from hempseed oil, flour, and meal, and we don't have a problem with those items; however, whole cannabis seeds, whether they are industrial hempseeds or marijuana seeds, are not excluded from the law. You cannot have cannabis seeds in your possession under any circumstances. Now, we understand that you were just using the seeds to sprinkle on top of some of your food items, and there has been no indication of you distributing the seeds for any other purpose, but nevertheless, those seeds are illegal. Here's the dilemma we're in—because there is a war on drugs, we are caught in a gray area. If the public's perception turns in favor of eating cannabis seeds, and they think it's a good idea, then it sends the wrong signals to law enforcement and the court system, and of course, we can't let that happen. It would be bad for morale and bad for the war on drugs."

Mr. Wright stood up and placed the palms of his hands on the edge of the desk, in an effort to make himself look bigger. Then he told me, in a stern voice, "The United States government is spending billions of taxpayers' money on trying to stop cannabis seeds from entering this country, and you're selling it in your food products. This is not open for discussion or debate; either you close your restaurant or we bring international, federal, and state drug-smuggling charges against you and your wife. The trial could be long and nasty, not to mention emotionally and financially draining. You've made several million dollars from the restaurant; now it's time to let it go. We'll let you keep the boutique. Sign the necessary paperwork, and we'll drop the charges and make a public apology. If you do that, we'll have you and your wife out of here by the end of the day. If you don't sign, we'll step on your throats and make your world miserable for the rest of your life."

I knew that he was right; we could spend a fortune fighting this unjust law, or we could get out of this nasty situation and go on with our live. The system was corrupt, and we aren't the ones who would change it. Maybe someone in the future would come along and write a book about it and make a blockbuster movie that would click on the public light bulb, but that remains to be seen. I was allowed to discuss the problem with my wife, and we both agreed that discretion was the better part of valor, and so we took the deal.

This story needs to be told, because the criminals in Washington are destroying the free-market system, and they are using the destruction of the hemp industry as a template to destroy the Constitution, academia, and the economy. But the good news is that the cannabis industry has won the war on drugs whether the government wants to admit the truth or not. Individuals, in massive numbers, are standing on their own two feet and ruling themselves.

A Secret That Hemp Knew Best

By Chuck Allen Jr.

Back in the days when hemp was king,
The value of the fiber was everything.
Canvas for sails that moved the ships
Gave hope to the captains to make their trips.

The world was conquered, the oceans were crossed;
Seeds must be saved, no matter the cost.
Hopes and dreams and plans and schemes
Were grown in the fields for kings and queens.

Back in the days when hemp knew best,
The value of the fiber was put to the test.
Clothes and shelter, medicine and food
Held armies together and brightened their mood.

Today the plant has been erased from the books
By doctors and lawyers and political crooks.
They know if the people had the right tools,
The leaders of this country would all be fools.

CHAPTER 11

The Secret Story of the Biggest Marijuana Garden in US History

When strong opinions are held to the light,
The cannabis plant will still be right.

I saved this story for last, because to me it represents the epitome of what this book is all about. If you have the burning desire, the undying determination, and the unrelenting courage that it takes to dedicate your life and your soul to the pursuit of making a million dollars growing cannabis in the woods, then this story is for you. I'm sure that in the past there were farms that grew hundreds, or perhaps thousands, of acres of industrial hemp plants for commercial use, but this story is not about the hemp industry that was destroyed over seventy-five years ago. It's about the biggest and most successful marijuana garden ever grown in the United States—and the DEA never had a clue what was going on. I'm sure there are similar grows that are happening today, but with satellite technology and airplanes with infrared camera surveillance, large marijuana gardens are left to only those brave pioneers who are still true to the industry and have learned to rule themselves. Of course, it helps to have balls the size of Texas. Once again, names and locations have been changed to protect freedom.

This story was told to me by a good friend who has since passed away. (He was fly-fishing in a river when he had a heart attack and left this world to go see the Great Fisherman in the sky.) My friend's name was Richard, but believe me when I say that no one ever called him "Dick," because he was six foot six and 260 pounds of solid grit. He had a big black, bushy beard that looked small compared to the width of his shoulders. In spite of his fierce and angry appearance, Richard was actually a kind and gentle man who was just as comfortable around women as he was around children. But don't mistake his tender nature as a sign of weakness, because Richard was a former Navy SEAL, and he was always two steps ahead of everyone else. His survival skills served him well in civilian life. He chose to become a professional butcher, and his knowledge made him more than capable of managing the largest meat department found in any supermarket in America.

Richard and I became friends while working at the same supermarket in California; he was the king of the meat department, and I was the star of the produce department. On days when the weather was too stormy for shoppers to venture out, we would tell each other jokes and try to solve the world's troubles over a cup of coffee. You could say I got to know him very well over the course of two years. Richard had a great sense of humor and didn't care whether you agreed with him or not. Just being around him made me feel grateful that I was his friend and not his enemy.

One time he told me that as a younger man he had played drums for a famous rock band from a southern state. He told me their name but asked me to keep it confidential, because he didn't want to draw attention to himself. The band sold tens of millions of records, and they all became wealthy. After the lead singer decided to go solo, the band dissolved, and the players went their separate ways. Two years later, Richard got married, moved to the California, and built a home in Sonoma County. The royalties from the band's records are still being automatically deposited into a trust fund for his family's future.

I was curious to know if his story was true, so the next time I was in Walmart, I looked through the CDs. I found his face on the front of one, and on the back was another picture of him playing the drums. The caption underneath listed all the other band members' names too. I was so excited about being friends with a famous musician that I bought all the CDs I could find, and today I still treasure those songs as if they are gold. But I never told him that I verified his story, because I didn't want him to think that

I didn't believe him. What I did instead was let him hear me whistling a melody or humming a tune from one of his songs while walking around the store. It was a secret bond of trust that we both understood and appreciated. Richard was the king of the meat department, and that was good enough for me.

There were times when we bumped into each other outside of work, like at restaurants, movies, or walking on the beach, and our wives became friends too. One time we went to their house for a barbecue on Super Bowl Sunday, and Richard got to show us what a good cook he was on the grill. But our families lived twenty-five miles apart, so our social activities were limited to special occasions, which made working together the perfect balance for a friendship.

Richard was a great outdoorsman, and hunting, fishing, and camping were his passions. He looked the part too. He could have been a frontier man, a pioneer, a mountain man; he would have been capable of surviving the harsh conditions of any wild country. But he loved his vodka and pot too much to get very far from his truck.

One night, Richard and I were cooking dinner over an open fire down by local river (trout, red beans, fried potatoes, corn bread, and coffee), and he started to tell this story about how he and some of his friends had made millions of dollars growing pot in the hills of northern California. He said that he hadn't needed the money but had done it for the adventure, because he thought growing marijuana in the wild was the last American adventure left in this "free" country. Too much civilization, too many titty-babies, too many scaredy-cats, too many excuses, he believed. In his mind, the world was divided into two types of people—those that did and those that didn't. In his opinion, most people didn't want to take a chance; they wanted the government and the unions to do it for them. So, there was no critical thinking from them anymore; they left it to someone else, who had a different agenda than most of the citizens. There were too many Progressives and too many extremists on both sides of the political spectrum, according to him. It didn't take a brave person to work for minimum wage and sink deeper and deeper into debt just because he was too fat, lazy, and spoiled to get up off his butt and change what he was doing for a living.

Richard said that he was throwing down the gauntlet to see what kind of person I was. Then he passed the pipe to me while blowing out a cloud of blue smoke big enough to choke an ox. With this sheepish grin on his face, he told me that he was just kidding, because he was sure that I already knew what kind of man I was. Besides, he told me, growing pot in the woods was a young man's game. He said that he wouldn't attempt it anymore even if someone paid him a million dollars cash up front, because he was too spoiled and happy to live in the wilderness for four or five months without his wife. He then suggested we build up the fire, fix ourselves a nice strong drink, and sit here under the stars in these plastic lawn chairs while he told the story of his first, and only, marijuana grow in the wilderness.

It's hard to say who had the idea first. There were four of us renting a beach house in Panama City, Florida, in the summer after the band broke up. We were young, rich, and carefree, and the beer, pot, and bikinis were flowing from day to day as easily as the winds and tides were moving on the shore. It was during the holidays in the last few months of 1968 that we started to think about what we were going to do with the rest of our lives. My best friend and his two brothers thought Panama City was the best place to start looking, and we were having the time of our lives. There was no need for any of us to rush into careers that would bring an end to the youthful freedom we were experiencing.

My best friend and his two brothers were Vietnam veterans, and the youngest had married a girl from Hanoi. Unfortunately for him, he was having problems with the military and getting her a passport, but fortunately for us, she was sending him pounds of marijuana to a post office box in Gulf Shores, Alabama. This little smuggling game had been going on for over a year, and we had plenty of top-grade buds and thousands of marijuana seeds.

On New Year's Eve, we were playing poker, getting high, and waiting for the big ball in the sky to drop in Times Square. We started talking about New Year's resolutions and what we were going to do to keep our agreements—knowing full well that no one was serious about any of it. Someone said (I think it was my friend Bob) that what he wanted to do was to grow a ton of pot and make a million dollars. The youngest brother jumped up and started bouncing around the room, screaming, "That's it! That's it—we can do it!"

As it turned out, their family owned a three-thousand-acre ranch way back up in the hills of northeastern California, adjacent to the Modoc National Forest, right on the three borders of Oregon, Nevada, and California. Their uncle was caretaker of the ranch, and he raised mules for sale and rent to various hunting and tourist organizations. It would be hard to find a more desolate and abandoned area of wilderness on the American compass, except perhaps for Death Valley and the Utah salt flats. Back in the late sixties, the DEA didn't have helicopters, infrared cameras, and multimillion-dollar budgets to spend on ground troops searching the forest for pot growers, but what they did have was undercover informers disguised as farmers, ranchers, hunters, campers, hikers, forest workers, biology students, bird watchers, photographers, prospectors, pilots, balloon enthusiasts, and people from any number of other walks of life willing to turn in their fellow citizens for 10 percent of any property seized in a drug raid. (Ten percent of a million dollars is $100,000—not bad work for just walking around in the woods or taking the family for a plane ride on the weekend.)

The good thing about the mule ranch was that the nearest neighbors were an elderly couple with no family, who lived twelve miles away to the south. They had no reason to suspect that the tough old mule rancher had anything to do with growing marijuana. That thought was probably as remote to them as the country they were living in. The county road ended at their property line, and beyond that there was no electricity, TV, radio, or refrigeration, except with the help of generators. People who ventured into that area of the countryside had to be mentally and physically as tough as a mule.

We spent the first two weeks of January 1969 making a list of everything we might need for our million-dollar garden in the wilderness. Food, shelter, clothing, and medical supplies topped the list. Then we bought topographical maps of the area and started to study potential grow sites that had adequate water and sunlight. The type of terrain we would be going into was mostly rocky low hills covered in scrub oak, manzanita trees, and black pine. The landscape was hot and dry, with few springs and even fewer year-round creeks. There would be no logging roads or jeep trails that we could follow but only deer trails, animal paths, and dry creek beds. We figured it would take six mules four days to go twenty miles into the wilderness (if we averaged five miles a day). Each of those five miles would prove to be a difficult and dangerous journey for both man and beast.

We realized that we needed to get into shape and stop drinking and smoking if we were going to be of any use to each other out in the boondocks. Our goal was to be in California within the next thirty days and then to spend two months gathering supplies and learning how to deal with the mules. By the first week in May, we should be in the boonies, prepping the ground for planting. We gave notice to our landlords and made financial arrangements to leave the Florida area.

The cost of this project was estimated to be somewhere between $3,000 and $4,000 for each partner. In reality it turned out to cost $6,000 for each partner ($36,000 for six months in the woods). We made up a food supply list for six men and six mules for six months.

We had to estimate how much food one person and one mule would need per day and then multiply that number by seven days, then by four weeks, and then by six months. That would give us the estimated cost to feed one man and one mule for six months in the wilderness. It didn't take us long to figure out that it was a huge problem to feed six people and six mules for six months in the boondocks—not to mention the logistics of transporting all that weight.

You have to understand that none of us had ever done anything like this before, except some military training in jungle and desert fighting. None of us had ever planted a garden or toiled the ground. We weren't farmers and we didn't know any farmers. We had to educate ourselves as we went along. We knew how to survive harsh conditions and what plants to eat or not eat, but as to how the food got on the table, we didn't have a clue.

Before we started to panic too much, we went to bookstores and libraries, searching for information about gardening and recipes for hunting and camping. We learned that it was most important for long-term survival in the wilderness to supplement our diet with fresh protein, like fish, deer, rabbit, or snake. That created another bag of problems, because we didn't know how abundant the wildlife was in that desolate area, being that water was so scarce.

Richard was the one who came up with a workable solution to the food and supply problems. Each man would have his own mule and would carry his own food, water, clothes, and shelter. He recommended that each partner carry a .22 revolver for protection against snakes and other critters and a pair of high-top boots to help protect against twisted ankles. The mules would carry supplies and their own feed and water. According to the topographical map, they would only have to travel ten miles into the wilderness to find a suitable water source, and that should be far enough to discourage anyone from looking for pot gardens. Our first trip out there would be for setting up camp, with the mules carrying tents, PVC pipe, hand pumps, tools, drinking water, and fertilizer. In his backpack, each man would carry enough food to last ten days, mostly dry food that could be prepared with hot or cold water (oatmeal, soups, beans, rice, dried fruit, raisins, nuts, instant breakfast, vitamins, coffee, sugar, candy, etc., etc.). Also, each man would carry his own first-aid kit with hydrogen peroxide and iodine.

When we got to the grow site, four men would start setting up camp, and two men would take two mules and return to the ranch to pick up more food and supplies. Two days to get there and two days to get back, with one day of rest in between. When they returned, we would rotate and do the trip again, until we had enough food and supplies at the camp. Once we had the camp stocked, we'd probably have to return to the ranch once a month to replenish supplies. We would use hammocks on the trail, make no fires, and leave no trash. We would make as little noise as possible and keep our eyes open for signs of trespassers.

Back in those days, we didn't have cell phones, so if someone got hurt it could be a life-threatening event. One broken bone, one slip of the knife, or one snakebite would take two men out of the ball game and possibly the chance to make a million dollars. This was a once-in-a-lifetime chance; it would never happen again. Needless to say, safety was on our minds every step of the way.

Dealing with mules is no easy task; they can hurt you without even trying. They kick, bite, stomp, stumble, slip, and fall, just like any other animal—except they do it with attitude. Even when mules are well fed and watered, they don't move unless it's their idea. They don't start or stop with someone else's command; they dance to their own tune, and just because you stop doesn't mean they will. This means that they will step on your heel or push you in the back and knock you down with no concern for your safety at all. So, being around mules requires that you be alert at all times and try to solve problems before they happen, not after. None of us had any training with mules, so we had to learn on the job, which was a danger in itself.

In the second week of April, all six partners arrived at the ranch, ready to start buying supplies and organizing the logistics of the marijuana project. We formed into teams of two and drove to different towns as far away as a hundred miles. We bought nothing with credit cards or checks, leaving no paper trail to link us with the supplies, just in case something went wrong at the grow site.

The uncle who lived at the mule ranch reminded me of Yosemite Sam from the cartoon: short, skinny, and bowlegged, with a long, droopy mustache and a hot temper. He loved the idea of what we were doing in the boondocks, and he was constantly cracking us up with his little quips like: "Going out there in the boondocks to get ayah-self some more fuel, are ayah? Better bring me back some, 'cause I'm a-getting low too." He called marijuana "fuel" and all he wanted in return for the use of his six mules was a few pounds of some good fuel. One time he came into the kitchen and proudly proclaimed that it was time to put some more fuel on the fire; then he lit up his pipe and passed it around. He was a tough old boot, but he had a wonderful sense of humor. We called him Uncle Sam, and he called us all by the same name—Butch. I guess it saved him some time for having to learn six different names if he lumped us all into the same basket. But we didn't mind; no one wanted to give out his real name anyway. Our project was one for all and all for one, so we might as well all have the same name. And it was kind of interesting too—we were a bunch of hardheaded guys responding to an old mule trainer who called us by one common name, just as he would a pack of mules.

Without Uncle Sam's help, our first attempt at being entrepreneurs in the cannabis industry would never have gotten off the ground. He gave us a crash course in Mule Training 101. How to feed, water, and keep them healthy. How to pack and unpack, how to get them started, and how to get them to stop. How to keep them from running away, and if they did, how to get them back without chasing them all over the countryside.

We weren't fooling ourselves and going into the wilderness unarmed; we took a .22 automatic rifle for deer, and a twelve-gauge shotgun for bear and pigs. Our sidearms were mostly for snakes, because we were going into the heartbeat of rattlesnake country.

Our first mule train left the ranch on April 19, and we made it to our destination three days later. Not knowing where we were going and not being experienced on the trail slowed us down considerably. But with practice our timing got better, and we were able to make it to camp in two days and back to the ranch in a day and a half. I don't want you to think that these mule-train trips were some kind of Sunday walk in the park, because they weren't; they were dangerously hard work. The heat and dust alone would make a normal man question his sanity. Then there was the frustration of the mules having their own ideas of where they were going and when they would get there. Everything we did was dangerous, tough work. Don't think for a minute that growing marijuana in the woods is an easy slide into home plate, because it's not. There's a big, bad player standing in your way, and his name is Mr. Luck, and you have to get past him before you can score.

We found a beautiful small valley, maybe five acres wide, with a deep-water creek winding its way down the middle. Our garden would be divided by the creek, with the ground gently sloped on both sides. We used the mules to till the ground and to work the fertilizer into the soil. After a few days, we spread the seeds and covered them lightly with topsoil. Our watering system was primitive but effective. We hand-pumped water out of the creek into plastic swimming pools, the kind you see in backyards, and used them as storage tanks elevated off the ground on platforms about six feet high. We used PVC pipes and water valves to regulate the flow of water to the garden sites. Within a week we had hundreds of thousands of sprouts, and within a month we had five acres of seedlings six to eight inches tall. By the Fourth of July the plants were knee high, and we started to mix Rapid Grow fertilizer in the water (one tablespoon per gallon). By the end of August we were mixing a fertilizer for blooms into the water to encourage the plants to produce more buds.

All the work was done in rotating shifts, with two men on each team: two men pumping water into the holding tanks, two taking the mules back and forth to the ranch, two cooking, two taking care of the mules, and two walking the perimeter of the garden looking for deer, etc. Each man had his own tent, air mattress, sleeping bag, coffee cup, toothbrush, mess kit, toilet paper, and hammock if he didn't want to sleep on the ground. The privy was a trench in the ground with a tarpaulin wrapped around three trees, located about fifty yards northeast of the camp. We always used flashlights at night because of the snakes. It would not be a good idea to get up in the middle of the night to go pee and step on a rattlesnake—it would be a nightmare come true. With food and supplies being brought into the camp once or twice a month, life in the wilderness wasn't that bad, except for the spiders, ticks, mosquitoes, and snakes. Did I say snakes? I mean *a lot* of snakes. It was a miracle that no one got bit, because there were snakes everywhere. At least once a day someone killed a snake—not always with a pistol, mostly with a shovel. Rattlesnake meat fried in vegetable oil and served with beans and rice isn't that bad when you're good and hungry! It tastes just like chicken that's been bitten by a snake.

Our biggest problem besides snakes was the deer eating the pot plants. They came around mostly at night or early in the morning, and we had to keep a constant patrol. It wasn't a good idea to be firing weapons in the middle of the night while people were trying to sleep, but we did shoot deer whenever we could, because venison steak was much better to eat than snake meat.

In the second week of September we started to harvest. Although the crop was seeded, the quality of the smoke was excellent. There was absolutely no way we could have culled out all the male plants, with the crop being so big. But our taste tests assured us that these buds came from some of the finest Thai plants grown anywhere in the world. None of us could have imagined in our wildest dreams how many buds we were growing in that five-acre chunk of land. As the plants started to mature, and the buds began to ripen, the idea that money grows on trees took on a whole new meaning. We now realized that fortunes and dynasties *can* grow on trees. It took six men harvesting ten hours a day for two weeks—before the weather started to turn cold—and we still didn't get all the buds. We packed two hundred pounds on each mule, and it took ten trips to the ranch before we had to stop. We estimated that we harvested a little over six tons, and I still dream about how much more we could have gotten out if the weather hadn't turned so nasty!

Each mule train returning to the ranch brought with it twelve hundred pounds of fresh-cut buds that needed to be dried. With the weather turning cold and damp, there was the problem of bud rot—more commonly known as mold. (That happens when buds get wet and don't dry out fast enough to remove the moisture.) Anyway, if we couldn't dry out the buds soon, we could lose the entire crop, and our adventure would be a disaster. Fortunately for everyone concerned, Uncle Sam had a huge barn, with two wood-burning stoves, to keep his mules warm in the winter. We covered the floor of the barn with plastic tarps and spread the buds as evenly as we could, about a foot deep, from wall to wall. Then we bought six oscillating fans and placed them around the barn. We turned the buds every six hours with leaf rakes. This process of drying took over ten days of constant hard work, with cutting and carrying wood and turning and raking the buds, but finally, when the crop was thoroughly dried, we discovered much to our surprise that we had harvested a little over *three tons* of fresh marijuana buds. And the project still wasn't over! We had to weigh out 6,000 pounds of dried buds into one-pound ziplock bags. It took four men, each with his own scale, filling 108 plastic bags every day, two weeks to complete the task. (That's 430 one-pound bags every day for 14 days.) Try to close your eyes and wrap your mind around 6,000 pounds of dried marijuana buds all piled up in the middle of a huge barn just waiting to be sold for a fortune. If you ever want to know what $12 million tax-free looks like, just go back and read the sentence before this one. That's as close as you will ever get to it—unless you have the courage and determination to stand up on your own two feet and rule yourself.

So, the perfect formula for making a million tax-free dollars growing marijuana in the wilderness is this:

There are 2,000 pounds in one ton. 2,000 x 3 tons = 6,000 pounds
6,000 pounds divided by 6 partners = 1,000 pounds per partner

1,000 pounds x $1,500 bulk rate for seeded pot = $1.5 million tax-free

Do the same thing again for the next 5 years, and retire with $7.5 million tax-free.

Do the same thing again for 10 years, and retire with $15 million tax-free.

The most important formula that you need to understand regarding the cannabis industry is this: if you can grow one pound, you can grow a hundred pounds; if you can grow a hundred pounds, you can grow five hundred pounds; and if you can grow five hundred pounds, you can grow a thousand pounds. A thousand pounds is all you need to grow to become a millionaire.

I'll never forget that night on the local river, with Richard telling me his story of guerrilla farming in the golden hills of northern California. He had already been a successful musician and had more money than the average lawyer; there had been no reason for him to grow pot in the boondocks. But he had had to prove something to himself, something that sold-out concerts couldn't provide—a feeling of self-preservation that had been lost in the crowds of adoring fans. It wasn't the gold records hanging on the walls that he needed. It wasn't the music, or the history books, or the fan clubs around the world. It was a feeling, a knowing, a river of strength that he was able to dive into every time he thought about his ability to self-rule. Maybe it was the understanding that he hadn't done it by himself— nobody does, not if they tell the truth about it. There is no such thing as a "self-made millionaire," only self-made men. There are ideas and products, and supply and demand. Someone besides the government has to buy into those concepts, or the free marketplace will implode and the republic will be lost forever. Richard believed with all his heart and soul that the cannabis industry was the last classic example of how a true entrepreneur could make a difference in the lives of his family and his country and prove to himself that he still had the values and principles necessary to rule himself. Of course, it still took courage and determination with balls the size of Texas.

For millions of music fans, Richard will always be remembered as one of the best drummers in rock 'n' roll history; and to thousands of residents in California Richard will be remembered as the king of the butchers; but to me he will always be a founding father in the Marijuana Growers' Hall of Fame and a true pioneer of the cannabis industry.

The Cannabis Plant

By Chuck Allen Jr.

When congressmen and senators lose their seat,
The cannabis plant will not retreat.
After the republic is dead and gone,
The cannabis plant will still be strong.

When the new world order has finally arrived,
The cannabis plant will still be alive.
After the dollar and the flag disappear,
The cannabis plant will still be here.

When pundits and pirates have sunk the ship,
The cannabis plant will still be hip.
After all the prayers have finally been sent,
The cannabis plant will pay the rent.

When food and water are hard to find,
The cannabis plant will come to mind.
After the madmen have found all the gold,
The cannabis plant will still be sold.

When strong opinions are held to the light,
The cannabis plant will still be right.
After lawyers and judges have poisoned the rules,
The cannabis plant will make them fools.

When a nation of people are no longer free,
The cannabis plant will be easy to see.
After the fat cats have eaten all the birds,
The cannabis plant will have the last words.

CANNABIS SECRETS
THEN AND NOW

Back in the old days there were no secrets about the cannabis plant. Everyone around the campfire knew exactly what it was and how it could be used. The local medicine man had his own special mixture of herbs and brews that he kept to himself. He passed the recipes down from generation to generation as a spiritual rite of passage from novice to master. The cannabis plant itself was no secret. The fiber of the plant was used to make clothes, shoes, rope, sails, rugs, twine, paper, and a variety useful products used in everyday household tasks. The stalk of the plant could be used for feed and bedding for livestock, and the leaves could be steeped in tea to reduce pain and help induce sleep. The seeds of the plant could be crushed into a dry meal and used to make bread and other healthy food items. The seeds could also be squeezed into oil and used for cooking and lamplight. There were no secrets about the usefulness of the plant, only the lack of knowing exactly how many thousands of other products the plant was capable of producing in the distant future.

Then something very interesting happened in 1753. The scientific community discovered the cannabis plant, and a closer look at the subject matter was deemed necessary. The plant was first "discovered" in northern Asia by a biologist named Carolus Linnaeus. He was the first scientist who classified the *Cannabis* genus by using the modern system of taxonomic nomenclature to identify plants. He considered the genus to be monotypic (having just a single species). Thus he named the plant *Cannabis sativa L.* (The *L* stands for Linnaeus and indicates the authority who first named the species.)

Thirty-two years later, in 1785, a noted evolutionary biologist named Jean-Baptiste de Lamarck published the description of a second species of the cannabis plant, which he named *Cannabis indica Lam.* Lamarck based his description of the newly named species from a plant that he had found in India. He described *Cannabis indica Lam.* as having poorer fiber quality than *Cannabis sativa L.* but a much greater utility as an inebriant. (In other words, the plant grew shorter but when smoked or drunk it produced a much stronger effect.)

Then, 139 years later in 1924, a Russian botanist named D. E. Janichevsky discovered a new species of cannabis plant in Siberia, which he named *Cannabis ruderalis Janisch.* And in 1929, another renowned Russian plant explorer, named Nikolai Vavilov, found a similar cannabis plant, which he considered a wild or feral cannabis plant. These two discoveries are now considered the early findings of the industrial hemp plant named Cannabis ruderalis Janisch.

Up until the beginning of the twentieth century, human beings benefited greatly from the cannabis plant, and there were no facts about the industry that weren't already known to the consumers and the free marketplace. New hemp harvester machines were being designed and built that would revolutionize the industry. New plastic from hemp oil was being manufactured that was ten times stronger than steel. New hemp fuel was being manufactured to use in cars and trucks. New hemp building materials were being developed that would make cutting down trees obsolete. Hundreds, perhaps thousands, of new products were poised to enter the free market, when something absolutely unexpected and unpredictable happened. Our government, with the help of big business, went behind closed doors and destroyed a perfectly happy and healthy hemp industry for no other reason than greed and power. They certainly didn't do it with the approval of the American people.

Now we find ourselves at the beginning of the twenty-first century, being ruled by politicians and businessmen who are nothing but well educated cowards afraid to utter the words *republic* and *constitution* in public. Because they are so arrogant, pompous, and greedy, we are now $17 trillion in debt to a communist country.

This will soon double to $34 trillion when the interest can't be paid for in a few months. Every branch of the Freedom Tree has been infected with a social disease of some sort, including the roots. The pharmaceutical industry is busy behind closed doors trying to duplicate natural plants so they can sell their synthetic products in a drugstore near you. The medical industry is busy treating symptoms instead of finding cures. Academia has failed to step up to the microphone and tell the truth about anything, especially the cannabis industry. The legal system is being bought off and corrupted by lobbyists in Washington. Computer chips in voting machines are easily changed and influenced to reflect different results. The economy is being run by a group of counterfeiters hired by pirates in the White House. Television has been taken over by a powerful mass-media propaganda machine that is so effective that the smartest person in the room can't admit that he has been conned. None of these problems are secrets anymore; they have all been exposed long ago for what they are, and yet none of us has been able to anything about it.

The next big problem facing our country is definitely a secret that our leaders don't want you to know about until it's too late for you to do anything about it. They have a plan to take over the cannabis industry by controlling every aspect of the business, from start to finish. First, they will decriminalize it by placing it under the umbrella of soft drugs, giving out civil tickets and fines according to laws already in place for alcohol and tobacco. Secondly, they will encourage and allow states that vote for legalization to pay for the new system with tax revenues generated from the new industry. Third, they will encourage entrepreneurs to buy farmland and give them low-interest loans to buy equipment for their hemp or marijuana farms. Fourth, they will develop processing plants and shipping plants to centralized areas inside each state. Fifth, the material that is to be used for medical or recreational use will be shipped to one location, and the material used for the hemp industry will be shipped to a different location (cross-pollination could decrease the value of both industries). Ultimately, the idea is to set up the cannabis industry like the tobacco industry or the timber industry.

Buds from the marijuana industry and fiber from the hemp industry would be processed on assembly lines similar to those in the automobile or fast-food industries. Marijuana cigarettes would be packaged twenty at a time and sold at a fair market price, somewhere around $350 a pack. That's approximately one joint a day at a cost of $17.50 each. Better-grade marijuana brands would bring in a higher price (excuse the pun). Raw plant fiber and seeds would go to various manufacturing plants, according to the products being produced, and sold to different outlets around the nation and/or world. Slowly but surely, after these industries became successful, the hemp industry would start to produce fuel that would help offset the cost of the petroleum industry. Jobs that are lost in one industry would be replaced in another. The $60 billion cannabis industry that's alive and well today would be impacted, but to what degree I'm not sure. Supply and demand is one thing, but quality and price are something else.

There will always be those people who will refuse to work for the government because of the government's collusion with big business. They know that so many honest, hardworking citizens went to jail over a lifestyle choice that the government is now trying to make a profit from, without apologizing for the damage that was done (for no reason except for propaganda and greed). On one side of the coin this sounds like a good idea, but the other side of the coin is: who knows what the government will let big business do behind closed doors? They let the tobacco companies mix hundreds of harmful and addictive chemicals inside each cigarette and then lied about it in front of Congress on live TV. What's keeping the special-interest groups from lobbying for vitamins, vaccines, or antibiotics to be placed in the cannabis material for the good of the consumer? And into whose pockets would the profits go at the end of the year when the taxes are paid? Could this be another long-term entitlement scheme for the poor, so the politicians could cultivate more votes?

I strongly suspect that the political spotlight is shining on the marijuana industry today because the government knows they have lost the war on marijuana. So they are now throwing a political bone to the potheads as a diversion away from the hemp industry. The special-interest groups are still trying to save face and not allow the hemp industry back into the other more lucrative spotlight called the free marketplace, where better-made hemp products would be in direct competition with inferior synthetic and artificial products. At the very least, they know the hemp profits would drastically reduce the bottom lines of the special-interest groups that are so deeply rooted in the collusion between big business and big government.

I believe that the marijuana industry is doing just fine without the government or big business interfering with the status quo. Decriminalizing the product is a major step in healing this country, but the government should stay out of the marijuana industry, because they haven't demonstrated to the American people that they have the capacity to balance the budget or to negotiate fair business practices within the boundaries of their own country, much less the boundaries of our allies around the world. They messed up the post office,social security, health care, and academia. What they are doing now is simply muddying up the water and confusing the public with their propaganda slogans of legalizing marijuana and their false medical-marijuana campaigns. What the government needs to do now is shine the political spotlight on the hemp industry and allow this country to compete with the rest of the world. American-made hemp products could provide renewable resources for food, shelter, clothing, and fuel for a nation of people who are starved for the affection from their own leaders.

EPILOGUE

Don't interfere with anything in the Constitution. That must
be maintained, for it is the only safeguard of our liberties.
—Abraham Lincoln

Most marijuana smokers aren't interested in pot growers or
what it takes to cultivate, transport, or market the final product.
They could be mildly interested in where it was grown, or how
much it cost, but how it gets from field to table isn't really their
concern. The supply-and-demand part of the business is part of
that don't-ask-don't-tell code that consumers are better off knowing
nothing about. The industry is self-regulating, and the consumer will
only pay a fair market value, according to the quality of the product.

It has been estimated that there are sixty million marijuana
consumers in the United States who use it either daily, for recreational
use, or for medical purposes. I would "guesstimate" that the number
is closer to a hundred million, if you count the number of people
who don't smoke but are working in the industry: manufacturing,
transporting, and marketing the product on a daily basis. No
matter how you slice the pie, that's a valuable product that has its
own supply and demand. It's not going to go away just because the
government and big business declare prohibition on the industry.

One of the biggest social blunders the politicians and
businessmen ever made in the history of this country was to declare
prohibition on alcohol, but it pales in comparison to the mistakes
they are making with their war on the cannabis plant. There's no
better word to describe their actions than to call them *fools*.

Let me ask you these questions: Which is more important to you, the Tiki Torch recall from Walmart or the price of gas at the pump? Should we use corn for fuel and raise the price of beef at the grocery store, or should we build electric cars and increase our coal consumption? Should we use natural gas in our cars or build more nuclear power plants to save energy? Should we drill more oil wells and continue to consume petroleum products, or should we choose another fuel source that has already been proven to be renewable and cost effective? Do you believe that our leaders are the best negotiators in the world and have built lasting friendships with the Arab world? Are you confident that the government has our best interests at heart?

Let's be honest with ourselves for a change: our leaders aren't the slightest bit interested in using alternative forms of fossil fuels, either now or in the future. They are milking a cash cow, and until the cow dies they are not going to think about buying another cow. Oh sure, they will play political football with biomass products, just to keep the public satisfied for the moment, but they have no serious intention of replacing oil and petroleum products for any reason whatsoever. They will do anything, say anything, and pay any price to keep cannabis fuel and cannabis by-products off the free market and away from the American consciousness. That's because they know that biomass-derived fuels can provide our country with all the energy needs currently supplied by fossil fuel. Don't take my word for it. Do your own research. They know that you are too lazy and too busy to find out the truth for yourself, and that's why we're in the mess we're in. We've put our trust in them, and they don't have our best interests in mind. They are only interested in keeping their shareholders happy and making a profit.

We need to look at the problem from a different perspective: It's not the union that's the problem, it's the union leaders. It's not big business that's the problem, it's the CEOs. It's not Washington that's the problem, it's the politicians with no term limits. It's not the vote that's the problem, it's the lobbyists behind closed doors.

There is some housecleaning to do, but your hands are tied and the blindfolds are firmly in place. It's not what you see that counts, it's what you don't see. It's not what the right hand is doing, it's the left hand you need to be looking out for. Everyone is subject to a good left hook, and the American people are being sucker-punched from the moment they open their eyes until they are knocked out again at the end of the day. So the question is: what are you willing to do about it?

There is no place to hide; we've all been placed in the same wastebasket with the cannabis plant and made to feel irrelevant and misunderstood. After all, they know more about how to rule our lives than we do. And we must never, ever, get the idea in our heads that the cannabis plant could be beneficial to this country in any way shape or form, because that's just crazy talk!

It's a tough situation for us to be in all the way around. We lost so much of our savings when the stock market collapsed. We lost the value in our homes when the housing market crashed. We can't find work because the job market is weak. And too many of us are in poor mental and physical health to do anything about it.

I don't have the words strong enough to say how much this impacts an individual or a nation of people. Our leaders have lost touch with their constituents, and the system has become poisoned with greed and corruption. One side blames the other, and nothing is getting done except the erosion of the Constitution. It's not enough to cut back on everything you can and thank God you have some savings, because those are going to run out soon, and then what are you going to do?

Big government is in bed with big business, and that collusion is actually creating an atmosphere of false beliefs, based on the idea that the citizens of this country aren't smart enough to rule themselves, and so they have to do it for us. The problem with this idea is that there are many groups of individuals who are even more powerful than our own government, and they have their own special agenda about who's going to rule the world. I know what you're thinking: *Here we go again another conspiracy theory!* but think about this for just a moment. When does a conspiracy theory stop being a theory and become reality? Who are the Feds, and why can't we see their books? Why is the IRS above the law? Why have the Congress and the Senate become irrelevant? If the president isn't running the country, who is?

If you believe that the president *is* running the country, then you haven't been paying attention. No one gets elected without debts and obligations to special interest groups, like the Trilateral Commission, the Council on Foreign Relations, the Bilderberg Group, and the Bohemian Grove group. Don't take my word for it—look these organizations up for yourself. They all believe that they can rule the world in one world government (or new world order), and they are making major strides in that direction every day. That's a fact, not a theory. Do your own homework and check it out for yourself. Don't rely on me or anyone else to explain to you what's going on. When the republic is gone, you'll have to explain it to your children and grandchildren, and they are not going to be happy about it. Find out who these people are and what their goals are. You'll begin to understand how deep the problems are in this country and how easy it was for a community organizer who has never been a city mayor, a state governor, or a successful business owner with little political leadership experience just happens to be elected to the highest political office in the free world.

You may ask yourself, *What does all this political mumbo jumbo have to do with the cannabis industry?* The answer is *everything*— because destroying the hemp industry was a test for the rich and powerful to see just how far they could go in imposing their fanatical prohibition laws, against the will of the American people.

You probably think that I am a babbling idiot, but if you take away only one thing from this book, I want you to let it be this thought: We have almost lost the seeds and the knowledge to save this planet. If we can repeal the unjust hemp laws, it would be a giant step in the right direction. The cannabis plant can make us self-reliant, by creating thousands of new manufacturing industries and putting hundreds of thousands of people (maybe even millions) back to work. All the jobs that would be lost in the oil industry, the timber industry, the synthetic-fiber industry, the paper industry, and all the other industries that are polluting this country—all of them—can be replaced by products of the cannabis industry. This is not a theory, it's a fact. It's the most coveted secret that big government and big business don't want you to know about, because if you found out what they were doing, then the light of truth would expose them for the fools they really are. Can you imagine what life would be like if we weren't being held hostage by the oil companies? Can you visualize our state lands never being clear-cut or harvested again? Can you wrap your mind around the idea that all of our nation's wants, needs,and desires can be managed by the cannabis industry? Remember this, if nothing else: democracy doesn't work unless it's honest. That's why our founding fathers created the Constitution and the republic, because they knew that a democracy isn't honest and it doesn't work.

The next time you vote, you can thank the pundits and the bureaucrats for failing to tell the truth about the cannabis industry. The next time you go to the doctor, you can thank him for not telling the truth about the medical benefits of the cannabis plant. The next time you go to the gas pump, you can thank the oil companies for polluting the groundwater and the air with all their toxic chemicals. The next time you go to the pharmacy, you can thank them for polluting your body with synthetic drugs. The next time you go to the grocery store, you can thank them for processing all the food with the artificial ingredients that you eat. The next time you send your kids to school, you can thank academia for removing the cannabis plant from the history books. The next time you go to church, you can thank them for not teaching that God made the cannabis plant for people to use to heal themselves. And the next time you have a chance to discuss the cannabis plant with someone who doesn't understand, have the courage to share your education and tell the truth.

So, there you have it—the choice is ours. We can continue to kick the oil can down the road, or we can choose to find a better way to live our lives. It truly is up to us. It's our Constitution, and it's our republic.

Unfortunately for the average American citizen, there is a growing number of misinformed and disgruntled people who hate the Constitution and don't understand what a republic is. They haven't been taught the history of communism and fascism. They believe in social democracy and think it's all about community organizing and the unions and redistributing the wealth, because there are enough resources to go around for everyone and the rich don't deserve what they have worked for. Progressive thought and political correctness have infected academia and the legal system, and the seeds of destruction have already been planted. These aren't hippy-dippy baby boomers too stoned on marijuana to march in the streets. These are five generations of spoiled kids who were brought up in very liberal families, with no consequences for their actions. These liberals only wanted their kids to have a better life than what they had when they were growing up. Now, if they can't provide it for their kids, then they demand that the government provide it for them.

You may ask yourself, *What does any of this have to do with the cannabis industry?* The answer is *everything*, because you and I have bought into the colluded idea that we can't rule ourselves, that we need big government and big business to show us the way, and that without them we would fail as a country. Well, my question to you is, how's it working so far? Can you honestly look around and say that our leaders have your best interest in mind? This might be the best place in the world to live, but if we don't wake up, it won't be for long.

WHAT YOU CAN DO

The first thing you can do is realize that you *can* make a difference and that you *do* have a choice in the matter. You can stand up and take a look in the mirror, because change starts with you, not with the government. Not everyone is interested in the cannabis industry or growing marijuana for a living, and that's fine, but in order to change your opinion about anything, you need to educate yourself about what you're doing. If you believe that this country is going in the right direction and that the system will correct itself as it has done in the past, and you feel confident that the Constitution and the republic are being protected by the politicians and bureaucrats, then by all means, go ahead and keep doing what you've been doing. You will keep getting what you are currently getting. If, on the other hand, you have a gut feeling that something is drastically wrong, then maybe it's time you seriously considered thinking outside the box.

If you decide that reforming the hemp laws would be a good place to start, then look for like-minded people and start networking to find out what you can do. Get on the Internet and research the subject; go to the library or the local college and find support groups. Talk about hemp to your family and friends; look at both sides of the conversation. Perhaps then you'll want to join efforts to put the issue onto the ballots or into the legislatures, where all can express their opinions in a straightforward manner. Write to your congressmen and senators and ask them to explain why the United States is the largest consumer of hemp products in the world but we don't grow or manufacture it here in our own country. Then ask them whether they would support an initiative to appeal the hemp laws.

The subject of growing marijuana to make a million dollars is always open for discussion, but it is strictly a personal choice, which requires a serious commitment to yourself and to those around you. The same thing can be said about your commitment to changing the hemp laws. It takes courage and determination, but the results could make a difference in whether or not your country remains the land of the free and the home of the brave. Remember this: only in America can you rule yourself, because once America is gone, someone else will have the rule.

In the next few pages, you will find two examples that we can use to solve America's most pressing problems: our Congress and the economy. Big government and big business don't want you to know how simple the answers are, because it would expose their collusion. They have spent billions of dollars trying to keep these solutions out of the media and will refuse to acknowledge that these answers even exist. Every time these solutions come to public light, they are politely recognized and then promptly disappear into legal quicksand, never to be seen again until another voice of reason speaks up. Their plan of action is a plan of nonaction. Their strategy is to ignore the strategy. They bury the answers under a ton of paperwork and then hide them in a million filing cabinets around Washington, never to see the light of day again until another unsuspecting soul comes along and hands them another solution to America's problems.

I came across these solutions while doing research for another book, years ago. I found them purely by accident, because I wasn't looking for answers on how to solve problems I was looking for reasons why we were having so many problems. It was by a process of osmosis that I found the solutions. Anyway, the answer to the economy was presented to the California State Legislature in 1984. It promptly disappeared in legal quicksand and has never been seen again. Twenty-seven years later, California is bankrupt and is still kicking the oil can down the road of unemployment. Big government and big business refused to listen to the people. California's new hemp industry could have saved them from economic implosion. It's just another example of the extremes to which they will go to keep you from knowing how foolish they are.

The solution to the problems with our Congresses has also been around for a long time; in fact, the answer was a legal procedure for many years, and it was working beautifully until the Progressives discovered that if they amended the Constitution and removed the legal obstruction it would give them more time behind closed doors to introduce their radical ideas into academia and the court system. Thirty years later they are reaping the fruits of their labor.

Recognizing problems and having a solution to those problems creates a much bigger problem, which the American people haven't been able to solve very often. Once a bad law has been passed, it's practically impossible to overturn because of the wealth, power, and greed it took in the first place to create the law.

However, I feel confident that in this information age of technology, people can network much better. They can take these solutions, pressure their senators and congressmen to put these answers back on the ballets, and vote the corruption out of the legal system "for the good of the people."

INDUSTRIAL HEMP INVESTIGATIVE AND ADVISORY

Task Force Report

Submitted to the California House of
Representatives on March 29, 1984

Request a permit from the Drug Enforcement Agency (DEA)
for California to pursue research on industrial hemp on test plots
at universities in California. University research on industrial hemp
should be undertaken quickly so that California is in the position to
capitalize on the market for hemp.

Publication Date: February 29, 1984 Recommendations

Based upon the review of literature and testimony presented
before the California State Task Force, the members find that
industrial hemp is a versatile crop. There is potential for industrial
hemp to be an important alternative crop in California. Underlying
any recommendations to investigate, permit, or promote the
production of industrial hemp. So that California does not lose an
opportunity to enhance its agricultural leadership in the United
States, the Task Force believes the General Assembly should act upon
the following recommendations.

A.) Redefine *Cannabis sativa L.* and the Cannabis and Controlled Substance Tort Act, to differentiate between industrial hemp and marijuana. Industrial hemp should be distinguished as having a level of 0.3 percent or less of tetrahydrocannabinol (THC).

B.) Redefine *Cannabis sativa L.*, in the Cannabis Control Act as above.

C.) Distinguish between marijuana and industrial hemp and remove industrial hemp as a noxious weed in the California Noxious Weed Law.

D.) Encourage Congress to make the necessary changes in the United States Codes: 21U.S.C.812(10), and 21U.S.C.841 to distinguish between marijuana and industrial hemp as they relate to production, possession, and delivery.

E.) Recommend the Drug Enforcement Agency (DEA) and the National Office of Drug Control Policy adopt a new definition of Industrial hemp and recognize a 0.3 percent tetrahydrocannabinol (THC) level as the standard for industrial hemp. Recommend the Drug Enforcement Agency (DEA) issue permits and make it legal to produce, possess, and deliver industrial hemp in the United States and internationally.

F.) Request a permit from the Drug Enforcement Agency (DEA) for California to pursue research on industrial hemp on test plots at universities in California. University research should be undertaken quickly so that California is in a position to capitalize on the market for hemp.

G.) Utilize the research capabilities at California universities, and allocate funding to: 1.) Conduct market analysis; 2.)Perform agronomic research that identifies the best growing conditions of hemp; 3.) Study methods of adapting of machinery needed for harvesting hemp; 4.) Establish viable seed stocks and germ plasm collections; 5.) Evaluate the incorporation of hemp in conjunction or rotation with current crops; 6.) Develop economic modeling of profitability, including fiber yields in different regions of California.

H.)Provide for regional informational meetings throughout California for law enforcement, state government officials, farmers, businesses, and the general public on industrial hemp.

I.) Investigate the availability of new tools to lower the cost to regulate and test industrial hemp.

J.) Adapt a resolution to urge the Drug Enforcement Agency (DEA) to work with the United States Department of Agriculture (USDA) to set up a program to certify hempseeds, regulate industrial hemp, and establish a protocol for commercializing industrial hemp in the United States.

K.) Encourage the Drug Enforcement Agency (DEA) to include state participation in the development of rules and regulation of industrial hemp.

L.) Set up a committee to evaluate and research infrastructure needs and processing capabilities for commercial production of industrial hemp.

M.)Support and fund the establishment of a certified seed bank and germ plasm bank for industrial hemp in California to supply hemp producers around the world, in order to capitalize on the growth of the industrial hemp market.

N.) Adopt a resolution to urge Congress to establish an aggressive new research program to update the knowledge fund of industrial hemp, seed production, and marketing.

THIS IS HOW YOU FIX CONGRESS

Congressional Reform Act of 2011

1. Term Limits. Twelve years only, with one of the possible options listed below.
   A. two six-year Senate terms
   B. six two-year House terms
   C. one six-year Senate term and three two-year House terms

2. No Tenure/No Pension. A Congressman collects a salary while in office and receives no pay when they are out of office.

3. Congress (past, present, and future) participates in Social Security. All funds in the Congressional Retirement fund move to the Social Security system immediately. All future funds flow into the Social Security system, and Congress participates with the American people.

4. Congress can purchase their own retirement plan, just as all Americans do.

5. Congress will no longer vote themselves a pay raise. Congressional pay will rise by the lower of CPI or 3 percent.

6. Congress will lose their current health-care system and participate in the same health-care system as the American people.

7. Congress must equally abide by all laws they impose on the American people.

8. All contracts with past and present Congressmen are void effective 1/1/12. The American people did not make this contract with Congressmen. Congressmen made all these contracts for themselves.

Serving in Congress is an honor, not a career. The Founding Fathers envisioned citizens' legislators. Serve your term(s), then go home and get back to work.

What we need now is to get a senator to introduce this bill in the Senate and a representative to introduce a similar bill in the House. These people will become American heroes.

A Secret Cannabis Poem

By Chuck Allen Jr.

A western plantation on a wilderness slope,
Hidden by timber and watershed hope,
Grows a cannabis farm clinging to life,
A garden of love from husband to wife.
Four generations of seeds in the ground,
Producing the buds that never were found.
Community leaders don't like to say,
But they are spending pot money, anyway.
Four generations of plants in the dirt,
Dusty old trucks, and camouflage shirts.
A shelter of plastic, a garden with glass
Are perfectly made for growing some grass.
The old-time growers and youngsters with heart,
Just having courage is the best place to start.
Growing outdoors has a romantic appeal,
But growing indoors is best to conceal.
A loss for the Feds is a win for the home;
The growers in town know they belong.
Nobody cares where the money comes from
When the crops are in and the harvest is done.
A western plantation, in a valley of trees,
A clear-flowing creek, deep to the knees,
A garden of flowers, ripe for the taking,
A home for the free the growers are making.

The best pot poem that ever was written
Is about a garden that never was hidden
From infrared cameras and satellite photos;
With GPS tracking, now everyone knows.